Gunn, K.

THE KEEPSAKE

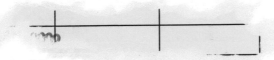

Also by Kirsty Gunn

Rain

THE KEEPSAKE

Kirsty Gunn

Granta Books
London

First Published in Great Britain by Granta Books 1997

Granta Publications Ltd, 2/3 Hanover Yard, London N1 8BE

A CIP catalogue record for this book is
available from the British Library.

1 3 5 7 9 10 8 6 4 2

ISBN 1 86207 013 X

Typeset by M Rules
Printed and bound in Great Britain by
Mackays of Chatham plc, Kent

Acknowledgements

The author is grateful for an award from the London Arts Board in the writing of this book.

For Merran

This is my memory, my own story with pale eyes. It is simple to tell, the story made for me, the story I make in turn to pass on. Nothing in these pages is lost in sleep, or in a bandage of pain. It is lived out in words and spaces between the lines that are like breath, a life formed as one word comes up behind the other, joins sentences that curve and change and turn back to face me on the page.

First Part

Sweet Cakes

ONE

The window, made of figured glass, gleamed. Around its base a broad band held the lead outlines of flowers and vines and fruits filled in with coloured glass, all the pieces within their lead moulds bright as jellies, and the thick glass plate above worked and bevelled so it caught the light and held it, turned prisms in the diamonds of glass and reflected back rainbows to the wall. That was why I visited the Portuguese café so often, for the coloured light the room held, the way it warmed the people who sat in it, gave lovely tints to their faces, pale rose and violet and yellow and blue.

Fernand kept the glass well polished for this reason; he was a business man. He knew how people who looked pretty in his shop would stay there and eat his cakes, as long as the light held, the warmth from the sugar and yeast rising. From out in the bare street, others would look in, be startled by how attractive everyone seemed. They would think how delicious the plates of cakes, how even the thick white china coffee cups looked like the kinds of objects a person would want to hold. The little diamonds at the edge of the window caught a fragment of passing sun and made jewels of the visitors' eyes. They glanced back through the glass and for a second saw everything in colour, like they were part of the pattern, like a ruby flower, like a clear green leaf.

There was a time when all the storefronts where I lived were as lovely, when all the wooden frontspieces were carved and set with glass, when the doors had brass bells that sounded one clear ring when a customer pulled the attaching cords. Now of the places I visited, only Fernand's café had such fine detail. He was proud of it, and in this way it was much more than financial sense that kept him polishing the flowers and fruit. He used to take a soft cloth to the lead edging with care, dipping a soapy sponge in and out of a bucket of hot water and wiping out the glass fruits with so much attention. It was not money he was thinking about then. The generous sweeping motions of his arms as he worked all over the glass described that, turning and swilling and spinning the sponge all over, steam rising from the glass, from the bucket, from him.

When the surface was completely coated by his sponge he went indoors, emptied the bucket and filled it with cold water, took it to the glass and sluiced it clean so every last trace of soap was gone, all the bubbles stripped away by cold water. Then with a rubber spatula he cleaned even this away, in broad clean lines, bringing the spatula down, from top to bottom, fitting each line to the next until no water was left only blade cuts, long ribbons of dry.

I saw him often at the window in this way, polishing the glass in the sun on a bright morning, his white sleeves rolled up against his dark arms, his breath coming out in puffs of cloud when the weather was cold. If he was not there, his boy was there, or another boy from the family. It was always like that, for as long as I can remember Fernand kept his café clean, all the years that passed until I saw it again and even then it was the same as before, the same little marble tables, wooden trays of cakes, and the glass as clean. My mother said it was a European way, to care for possessions, take pride in ownership and make your things so nice. There was the way Fernand's hand caressed the line of his counter when he spoke to her, put the coconut cakes she bought from him into the white paper bag as if they were fragile things in his hands to be kept perfect for her.

My mother loved his shop.

She loved to stand at Fernand's counter and let him pick out his best cakes for her. She wished she could be like him, use her palm to clear a surface clean, handle plates and glasses as if they were gifts or newly bought. She wanted to be able to give me food the way he did, dusting flour off the favourite loaf, using the best knife to slice out a piece of dark moist cake. It was European, she said, and European ways she loved because they reminded her of my father and she had always loved him the best.

In her memories of that man were all her fairytales of an old country, a huge foreign continent, way east of where we lived, across miles and miles that unfolded along centuries. From flat sand lands to high sierras where dry grass grew, on to rain soaked pampas, to brittle mountains with sharp stones scattered along the side of the road, created by ice, sluices of snow. Down through green paddocks, and lavender moors, through village squares in the south, where yellow baked churches chimed midday from low towers, past dark bars and cafés where flies dozed and buzzed against the clay walls, further east, and further, to where roads interlink at one-pump gas stations and lead out to half-empty industrial plants by the sea, to deserted factories standing in the middle of a field of sunflowers, further east again to where the grass darkens to blue and grows in a thick close pile, like velvet lengths running along the flat plains on either side of the river, miles and miles, and still it goes on, her lover has pulled down that dense, velvety blue, and there finally in the distance are the frightening spires, the twisted crosses on the cathedrals, the daggered points of black roofs, cruel silhouettes of castles, tall empty houses. A flock of tiny birds, like pin-pricks, are in the violet twilight sky above the city and as you draw closer you hear them crying, "Home! Home!"

Here was a land so familiar, a place that had bred a man in it so familiar to me. My mother could never stop telling me about my father, and how he loved the place he'd come from, was so blackly proud of the cold, the pebbled streets, the dark church lit by candles' flames that leafed the damp walls gold. He had those ways, my mother said, like Fernand had them, from his birthplace. They were there in the way he would take up a dried leaf from the table and present it to her as they sat together outside in the sunshine in the first weeks of their short marriage, in the way he ran his finger like a blade down the side of her fine face when he looked at her then.

All my mother's stories were like this, deeply known to me by heart. So closely printed that when I found a lover for myself, I had the writing in me already that he would meet me in a European café, talk to me there in queer half American, with a guttural tongue. I could have been her that he would choose to give me sweet cakes that first time, pick up a fallen lump and press it into my mouth.

"Take it," he said.

"Swallow . . ."

There was the way he tapped his black boot under the table, picking out the rhythm of a song only he could hear and I could have been my mother too in the way I also tried to hear it.

What was that phrase your father used to use?

I see her now, her head inclined as though she is listening for his voice in the air.

What was the word he used for love, just for me?

"You think I'm ugly now," the man said, "and old . . . But that will change . . ."

He leaned over and ran a finger down my cheek, down my throat. "I think you might like me. Really, I think perhaps already you do."

Inside the café Fernand always presided, he was proud and had to be there, serving personally if he could. Even if my mother came in for only one small vanilla roll he himself liked to pick it from the pile for her with his silver tongs, wrap it in thin paper with the edges folded under so it was a little package she could hold. Sometimes when she brought me in there, on one of her special days when she was spending the morning outside, or the afternoon, and we chose a table to sit at by the window, then Fernand would serve her that way, too, as someone who would wait, attend. He spoke with her as long as she needed, standing tall and courtly above her and as their voices murmured together I let the light reflections from the window play with my hands, turning them from crimson to purple. I opened my hand and held a piece of yellow light there in one palm, lilac in another.

After a time, Fernand would leave our table then return with the tray. In the same tradition he personally served my mother her black coffee, poured from a gold jug into a red cup so small I could have given it to a doll. On the red saucer lip he had placed a tiny paring of lemon rind, hanging like a fingernail at the rim. "For extra strength," said Fernand. "For bitterness."

I remember then when my mother's coffee was laid out, he passed me a plate of yellow cakes, special cakes for children because they were decorated with coloured sugar, pink and green. There was a fizzy drink for me too, that he poured into a long glass like a grown up, with a little packet of sugar, and a spoon with a jewel on the end to stir it with.

How clever I felt, on those days, to have all the pretty things before me. At home I was never fed meals on plates or given sweet foods, my mother didn't think of them. In the café, Fernand said "Let me give her a little treat," and she allowed it, but at home I ate the foods she made, or sandwiches from school or we had buttered biscuits. She had brought me up on her own, with no help from a family, and I learned early not to ask her for sweets and candy drinks when she never took them herself. I was used to that, and besides I was young and her sweet milk probably still ran in me, mixed with my blood. I had enough in me to make me grow.

My mother used to hold me up in the air for Fernand to see.

"Look how big she is, Mr Montale!"

On those days, when she was excited, she would get out of her chair, come around to me and pick me up under the arms and lift me towards him.

"I can barely hold this girl . . ." Her voice would be crying out. "She's so big now, she's grown, don't you think, Mr Montale? Don't you think?"

Her eyes would be bright and wild but Fernand knew her very well, he knew what to do. Instead of saying anything to my mother he just took me from her, set me back down in my chair.

"My little lady . . ." He broke the cakes on my plate and put one piece into my hand.

"Eat now. I made these especially for you . . ."

Then my mother returned to her chair, she was quiet again. She smoothed her hair. I bit into my yellow piece, the sugar sprayed on my plate like brittle rain.

"Look how she is," said Fernand to her, looking at her.

"Look how hungry . . ."

But my mother looked down, took her eyes away from him. She sipped her coffee.

Fernand was good with children because he had so many of his own, he was used to them all. My mother felt young and uncertain next to his sure touch with me. When he kissed me I felt he was my father, he reminded me of my father, like all men reminded me of my father. Like my mother said they did. She was always whispering to me, after her men friends left our flat, or sitting at the table in the café after Fernand had gone, "He reminds me of your father."

Even then, when I was too young to feel anything, still I didn't want to know her secrets. I traced with my finger the flower and stem pattern reflected from the coloured window glass clean onto the table. The colours were pale green and blue.

"He reminds me of him very well," my mother used to say.

"You know that, don't you? You can tell by the way I look at him that my feelings towards him make me remember that first time with your father. I can remember it, with Fernand, men like him, or with the others . . ."

I traced with my finger the same design, over and over. It was a pattern that was easy to do, stem to petal and around, petal back to leaf. Pale green and blue.

"I want you to listen to me," my mother whispered. "I want you to hear how I loved your father, how he loved me. How he made me feel. I want you to believe me: we were happy, all the time we had together. I don't mind that he's left us, and you must never mind, you must listen. You must remember: I was your daddy's darling . . ."

Her whispering became louder and louder until it wasn't like she was whispering, more like she was talking with something caught in her throat, an infection in her throat, her voice hoarse and rasping, and her bright eyes.

I looked down at the pattern I was tracing stem to petal and around. The colours were pale green and blue.

After she had finished her coffee we would go to the counter. When I was a little older I kept the money, I looked after it in a purse, but in the early years my mother could still manage it. Her cheeks held two spots of colour as she thanked Fernand for such a lovely time again, as always, such a lovely, lovely time. Kindly, he went and fetched our uneaten cakes from the table and wrapped them up for us to take home. He always told her to put her purse away.

All the time my mother's voice chatted on and on, it was as if she could not leave her place at the counter, other people had to wait behind in turn, waiting for her voice to finish and for her to leave. "I love coming to this place, I love it here. It's so very European, it's so pretty. You're so kind, Fernand. So dear to me . . ."

Fernand reached over and gently, gently took her hand.

"Everything is fine, darling. But you must go home now, you know that it is time." He kissed her hand.

"But come back very soon, promise. Au revoir."

Then he turned away from her, it was the only way she would leave.

"Now who is next?"

He was kind with her. No matter how long she lingered with him, pretending to decide to buy more cakes, or pretending to choose a jar of sugar fruits, he was polite, he gave her his time. She prolonged as long as she could the moment when she could look into his dark eyes, when he would finally say "*Au revoir*", the two foolish spots of colour on her cheek by then bright and burning.

"I don't know what to have, it's all so very nice."

She moistened her lips but she was pretending, she was only pretending.

"I wonder, I wonder . . ."

All the time Fernand was a gentleman with her, with no loud words, only kind sentences.

"I have a lovely strawberry tart today, my Marianne . . ."

My mother cast her eyes down like a girl.

"I have something with a coconut crust that I know you will adore . . ."

And my mother took short breaths, persuading herself that she had love again, that this man was like the husband she used to know, and I was trying not to listen, holding on to the paper packet, looking down at my shoes. My mother was already so sick, unhappy. Already she was taking the powder in small dosages that would later kill her.

*

Just as we never had to pay for our cakes in those far-off days, and when I returned to the café years later, and I was the grown one by then, still Fernand would not let me pay. I was in his shop twice, maybe three times, to order milky coffee and he pushed the change back at me over the marble table as if I was still a little girl. It was the only reference to the past he gave, not taking my money. He never spoke of my mother, or of the daughter she kept with her, down by her skirts. He never reminded me who I might have been. Even when I met the man in his café who would take me in, and give me food, and keep me in a bed as my mother had been kept, even then, Fernand never took my money.

Instead, he simply came to stand by my table.

"There is a man here who would like to meet you . . ."

His voice was the same gentle voice as before.

"I don't like him," he said, he didn't move at all.

"He is much too old. I don't want you to go to him . . ."

I looked over and saw a man with a brown painted face sitting on his own at a corner table.

"But I follow my instructions. This man has been looking at you. He says you carry a certain face. He sends these cakes to you . . ." Fernand held a platter of brightly iced pastries in his hand.

"These sweet things are his introduction."

Two

When you are alone for much of the time, even when you are young, memories are your lovers and companions, memory the skin on you, the hairs prickling the back of your neck when you're frightened, the quiet songs you hear when you're trying to sleep at night. Memory becomes your thirst, and hunger, all your appetites coming out of that same past place. Yet as you try to remember, as more and more memory is all you have, that's when memory leaves you. Even though you are young, still it leaves you and only details are left.

Details can be enough, though, for a person who stays alone. They will come alive. Like insects, tiny pieces of my memory team and swarm, one bright humming bit after another, suddenly, hundreds of them. There are the shoes I wore for my first day of school. Sentences in books I have loved. There, I remember the powdery taste of a biscuit eaten late at night. The white print of my mother's face in the darkness when we sat together in our room.

*

I remember that day in Fernand's café, the way the man sitting in the corner was still, like he was listening. His lips were red and unmoving and I thought how his body underneath his black clothes could have been made of thin bones and wire.

"I don't want him here," Fernand was saying, and he turned to the man, raising his voice so he would be able to hear.

"I don't want him here in my clean place . . ."

Still the man sat in the corner, listening to Fernand, waiting. He had black eyes, glass eyes. He rested over the table, sitting hunched over so quietly, not moving at all, listening, like a puppet . . . But much more clever. Like a puppet he could look so broken without the strings, his body limp, face fixed in a half-smile. But any minute ready to jerk up into life, his head swinging at the end of his long dark suit.

Ha! Ha! Ha!

I remember how, even as Fernand was still talking, I stood up, how I walked towards the strange man in the corner, and how suddenly he came up off the chair, all in a piece. His thin body was already beside mine.

Ha! Ha! Ha!

He took my arm, and he was not made of paper then.

"Come . . ."

His white fingers were like pincers.

"I've known that old auntie for years and years and years," he said, and he sat me down beside him.

'Don't take any notice of him, honey. Stay here and talk with me . . .'

These details are what I must content myself with now – the parts, because the rest is gone. Who was my teacher at school, what were the names of the books I read there? I remember the room I lived in with my mother and how quiet we were in the room together . . .

"Darling . . ."
She used to stroke my hair.
"Darling . . ."

We were in our room together, and it was warm in our room . . .

"Darling, my own little girl . . ."

Before the iced cakes, the mottled hand resting beside them on the table . . . Before anything else, there was my mother.

The hand came on me, the fingers wrapped round my arm . . . But before anything else, before him . . . It was always her.

THREE

When I came back to the city after many years away, I only wanted to be with my mother.

I was no longer a child but I wanted to stay with her, be with her. I wanted to go back to the house, find the room we had lived in together, push open the thin door, go inside and live there quietly amongst her things. I wanted only my mother's air around me, like breath, only her memory to swallow me whole in the dark. This dream was my comfort then.

It was autumn, it was a cold season. I had come back to the place where I had grown up, but I was a stranger there. Though the market streets were the same as I remembered them, every turn so known to me since childhood, I didn't feel familiar. My narrow shoes tripped in the gutter, my coat flapped open in a sudden breeze and I stopped, not remembering, not seeing. At shop windows and vegetable stalls I felt the round edges of my money deep in my pocket, but I was unable to buy.

I wanted to go back where I was safe but every day was the same. The sky hard and blue like slate with a sun that had no warmth in it, only good for a cruel kind of brightness that put edges into people's smiles, flashed silver off knives and bicycle spokes and locks, and made long black shadows form in the places where it didn't shine. There was nothing for me to do but walk, nothing to do but try and let the turns in the road hold me, open themselves only to me.

Sometimes the market was so busy that it was easy to become part of the crowds that separated and joined there, forming groups and patterns in the street and I felt better then, amongst them. The hippies and New Age travellers who sold scented candles and pot-pourri and rugs embroidered with Indian gods sometimes called me darling, and even the vegetable men allowed their fingers to touch mine as if they intended it, and the butchers, and the fish merchants with their silvered palms. In the brief autumn sunshine the travellers dozed on hessian rugs, bicycle messengers pulled up their cycles next to a lamp-post and leaned against them, lifting their faces to the thin warmth, closing their eyes against it. During those days it felt like all of us could have been sleeping, waiting. Like I wasn't the only one.

Time passed in minutes, hours, I walked up and down, past shops I remembered, past the cheap stands. In the morning the road dipped into a ditch of fish wagons and shish carts and slatted tables arranged around boiling tubs of sour soup from Thailand, or China, or vats of scented pork knuckle from Singapore. Later, the buildings pressed up closer and closer to each other, only leaving room for a small car to pass between them, or a couple walking arm in arm.

Hours counted off into days. There was the shop selling swags of velvet blouses, incense sticks, and long strings of coloured beads. There was the stall that sold foreign lettuces, red bulbs veined with white and curly black leaves wet and clean like freshly trimmed hair. In the late afternoon walking this way was to walk into a frozen northern light. Shadows formed in dark patches between the buildings, at night iced into slicks. A cold wind came down the hill and I wanted to walk faster, to cheat it, but it was no good. Every day I had to stay out until the light faded and night came. Only then could I stop, rest. Only when I could find myself back at the place where I wanted to be.

Towards the end of the day the vegetable and fruit market were still busy but it was too early then to go there. It was a sad time to be in the streets alone, that feeling you only get in cities when there's not much time left to sell, nothing much left to buy. Shops had switched on their bright lights, and stall-holders the strings of electric bulbs that swung above their heads.

"Cheap carrots!"

"Best tomatoes!"

They were closing down, the market was closing. All the money was running out. "Quick! Last chance!"

"Everything left got to go!"

I didn't want to be with people any more, their faces were cruel in the yellow light, their eyes were shadows, but it was not yet the time to go home and so I went on. Past the bakery with left-over buns decorated with cherries and white icing; past the man I remembered, who always sat outside the filthy supermarket with a fresh puppy under his coat to keep warm and get money from tourists. I recognised, too, the travelling girl who left her van at the end of the road all week-end and sold soap off the back of it, a hundred different kinds of soap I used to believe, pale pink and lemon and vanilla tablets stacked between tissue like confectionery. I used to buy it for my mother.

Gradually, these small pictures came back to me, the puppy, the scent of the soap. The rustle of thin paper. In the past there had been a baby with the travelling girl, it was a tiny baby, but as I approached the van I knew it wouldn't be a baby now. The girl herself was changed by age, her skin browned like a winter leaf, and her body hunched and hardened in shape by the weather.

I wondered if I would talk to her, if she would ever in this world believe me as the child who had given a finger for her baby to hold, who had kissed its cheek. The years had closed in on all of us, the baby grown up and near my own age by now, and the girl an old woman standing by the van, her soap not so special. Suddenly all I felt was cold, the light gone out. Of course she would not know me, there was no one here to know me. I walked past the woman, while her head was bowed, counting money, I slipped past.

It was getting dark, night had come.

One by one the shops closed up, pulled down their grilles, locked doors. The market traders packed away their crates, leaving their barrels and stalls empty behind them, unlit, but I knew the way like in a dream. Occasionally my eyes fixed on detail again, a cat gnawing at a piece of bone, or I saw someone's thin form behind a shop window, the owner perhaps, or a cleaner, looking out over the street smoking a cigarette . . . Still I kept on.

I walked on past the flyover, further on up the hill past the Spanish monastery with brick walls so high nobody would be able to see if there were endless gardens behind them, or cells. Past the intersection, and the Victorian iron palings of the underground toilets, where the light burned all night to save the eyes of the tiny attendant who lived there, further on.

I crossed over the road and finally there it was again, the same part of the street, the same house I had lived in with my mother all those years ago, the house I had always known I would have to look at again, to see, to remember . . .

It was deserted now. Gutter water ran down the outside walls like tears.

I could never live there. No one could live there. Though no placard showed it For Sale, though there was no sign of the demolition men who come to empty buildings, one by one, to remove and drag away in bits the inside walls, the cupboards and the pretty door . . . The building was condemned. The men could come and go and remove its poor inside parts and it would make no difference. It was already lost.

My mother had only rented one room of the house, with a kitchen off to one side, and a shared bathroom out on the landing. I guess the whole building was never well-kept, at the poorest end of the road, and the stucco front chipped and scabbed, with blisters of paint that I could peel back like skin if I wanted . . . Still, it was more forlorn than I could have ever believed. When we lived there together our room had been warm, without stains, or damp, Mama's sofa with her pretty rugs draped across it, our bed in the corner. I didn't think it was bad then, I didn't think it was bad for me. Yet when I looked up at it in those cold nights in early Autumn, it seemed the sort of home that could have the saddest memories. A closed-off room that could collect drugged sleep, and tears, and loss of love, like a chest.

Now, not even a stranger may have believed people could have ever lived there. Rubbish mounted the front steps that were cracked and broken, ornamental trees gone wild, blundered into growth, and everywhere weeds, snaking branches and harsh serrated leaves. Even if I'd wanted to walk up to the front door, to lean upon it as if it had been home, or as if I might go inside, I could not have forced my passage through the compacted thatch of leaves and stems.

The railings along the front of the house were half pulled down and more weeds wound around the iron bars, pressing to get through. In the dark, with the sodium street light casting twisted shadows, the sinews and tendrils of plants and giant faceless pods took on animal form, or human, all of them alive and clawing and clamouring to escape.

Let me go . . .

I wanted to turn and run when I saw this change, to get away from what time had done . . . Yet every night I found myself standing there, looking up at the house, up to the first floor where the window of our room gaped wide open to the dark air like a mouth.

Once more I was there, unable to leave that place. Once more it seemed, as I looked up, I was inside the room again, a child, standing there at the window, and I could feel at my back the familiar sofa, my mother lying upon it sleeping.

There was the touch of the cold glass, the shiver.

Let me go.

Four

I remember I used to stand at the window and dream of flying out into the air.

At night, the room became so small.

And I stood at the window I felt there was no space behind me and I could hear my mother in her sleep, I could smell her. I remember . . .

Don't do that, mummy. I don't like it when you do that to me.

I remember my mother undressing me slowly, lifting me, she carried me to the bathroom and placed me in the warm water, the bath-tub was filled . . . I remember our bathroom was on the landing outside our room, she had to carry me through a dark passage to get there.

It was cold, but the water in the bath-tub was warm and I was placed in it, so gently, like a gift. My mother soaped me all over with her bare hands, then she used a soft flannel to smooth the soapy lather into my skin, turning me, wiping me.

*

Don't do that mummy . . .

She wiped me, and soaped me. Her hands in the water were large and bare. They came under me, and around me, and the water was warm and soapy, and I was warm, becoming clean for my mother because she was making me, she was cleaning me . . .

"Your father lives very far away," she was saying. She smoothed down my body with the soap, then took the sponge, loaded it with warm water and squeezed it over my shoulder, my thin chest.

"Far away . . ."

Her hands were coated with wet, in the lamplight coming through the dark window they shone.

"He will never come back for us, but that doesn't mean he doesn't love us . . ."

She squeezed the sponge again and water trickled down again over me.

"You and I are his family. No separation, no distance, can undo him from his family. He loves us, you must believe that. You must believe me."

All my childhood we lived in a room for a home, eleven years and now I can't believe it was so long, when the memory of it takes up no space at all. I remember my mother kept the curtains in our room closed all day and only when the sky deepened into dusk did she open them, she parted them slightly to let the dark light in. Later there was orange in the dark from the street lamp outside, and sometimes my mother lit a candle, or purple incense that burned in fruit, but there was no other colour.

I think we didn't do anything together that needed much light. I think she read to me sometimes, or read to herself. She rested on her sofa.

She had soft pale-coloured rugs on her sofa, for sleeping, but there was a large skin there too, folded across the back. And I used to stroke it.

"There, there."

The skin was a keepsake, my mother said, and I used to wonder, when I was a child, if that meant that for the poor animal's sake we must keep it. Though it was dry, though the underside was flaking in cracks and lines like a flap of dried meat, she kept it close.

"There, there . . ." I used to say, as if it was a live thing.

"There, there . . ."

In the parts where it had not worn through, hairs were brushed close together in a nap, dark brown to black, and even though the skin was stiff to touch, and dead, my mother kept it close. It had been a present from my father and once, she said, he had placed it around her shoulders as though she was a princess and he would turn her into a queen.

She lived amongst all the memories of him this way, as if they were newly taken.

The skin was there on the sofa as if it was some fresh gift, not dry and worked in with dust, and in the bathroom she had his shaving things, the rusted blade and bone handle of the razor lain down on the bench as if, any moment, he would come in and pick it up. In the wardrobe were still hanging some of his clothes. A jacket was there in the dark, swinging like a dead man on a hanger, and there was a paper silk robe still faintly scented with cologne, and my father's shoes were there, set on the floor beneath the clothes, with creases in them where the leather had stretched to fit perfectly over the shape of his feet.

Often my mother used to go and stand in the wardrobe amongst the discarded clothes and slip her bare feet inside the oversize leather, the brown flapping tongues of my father's shoes licking at her ankles. She allowed the rough fabric of the hanging jacket to brush her cheek.

"I adore, *Je t'adore* . . ."

That's what she said then, her favourite words, the same whisper I heard in the dark, night after night, and I knew she was thinking about him, only about him, and her thoughts became more enclosed, dense, more heavy her breathing. Breathing deeply, going into herself, in deeper, deeper, thinking only about him, and the feeling of him.

These things were in me then, even when I was so young I didn't speak, these words were in me, in parts, slips, but filling me up.

"Your father lives far away . . ."

"But he'll come back one day, to claim his possessions . . ."

"He'll come back for us . . ."

For my mother, her stories were all her words.

Her whole language told her story, of the man who took her and then, after his daughter was born, went to some other place where she could never find him. "Far away . . ." she said, as if it was the ending of a story but there was never an ending for her. The words continued

34

to turn for her, and turn and turn. They need not have been her only memory, but my mother had nothing else in her to sustain.

Since she'd been a little tiny girl with long red hair she had had no strength and, now that she was old, sickness was in her. Whatever she took for her body had made her mind unwell, as if the pills and powder and clear liquids she burned for the needle had given her addiction as remedy for her stories, but in the end addiction only made the stories stay. She would never give them up. The past had become her. She was nothing else. Even with the use of the small packets of money that her family sometimes sent in the mail, she could never have left the room she had once shared with her only, her first, lover.

Yet though he was everywhere for her there, in her talk, in the strange things he'd left her, in her fretful secret dreams in bed, there was nothing for me. There were no pictures of my father, no little tufts of hair that I could tuck into my pocket. There were no papers with his name, no records of his height or weight marked down on a chart . . .

All I had for truth was my dreaming mother.

You have your father's hands . . .
Your father was such a tall man . . .
There was a certain way your father turned his head . . .

It was as if she was too bound up with his memory to care that even their wedding certificate, even the register for my birth with his name on it was gone. She alone was to be his proof of existence, the colour of his eyes were changing stones only she could keep. His body a reflection in moving water no one else could see.

Perhaps that is why, with such jealous knowledge of him that she couldn't let go even a piece of him to me, a handkerchief, I began to make up stories of my own. What my father's life was like before I was born, where he lived with my mother, in what countries, cities . . . These things I could imagine, make up foreign lands and two lovers travelling across them by car or by train, or by riding dark horses over endless plains with no roads, no change of air, only the sound of hoofs under a flat, flat sky.

Sometimes there was no foreign country, no fairytale at all. Then my parents kept themselves behind painted shutters and a clipped hedge, shyly making love together in a suburban house. Or they lived in an apartment with high ceilings, and undressed beneath a chandelier that didn't glitter in the grey morning light . . .

But most times the stories began as my mother told me. How they lived together in the same small room. How, from the beginning, she kept him with her all the time, charming him with female scent, and red hair, and all her rich parties.

I see my mother in those years, a young, young woman. She had no stained lipstick then, or dyed ends of a lost hairstyle. Then I see her hair as dark, dark red, gleaming as cherry-wood, her face smooth as though a person had taken cool soapstone and made her from it. Her long thin arms like a dancer's arms. Her perfect lips painted crimson because now she is fully grown.

"I don't think you've met . . ."

"Have I introduced . . . ?"

I see her, I do see her, beautiful and shocking. A young English girl from a family, a house, and all these people could be her friends, these people in drawing-rooms, and in dining-rooms, at dances, in draughty halls and ballrooms where the girls' silk dresses are not warm enough for them. So many people and here my thin mother stands with this man, this dark man from Poland, or Austria, or Russia, this big man who puts his face close to others when he talks, so they see themselves in his dark eyes but never him, they never see him entire, never see whether he is handsome or ugly or old.

He smiles, and my mother simply lifts her mouth towards him, to be kissed.

That's how a love affair was played then. Every gesture she made came from films, out of books . . . She was so easy for him to get. So easy for him to have her part her silken painted lips, smile for him . . . It only took a song, a close dance. It only took the curl of his finger against her bare skin, in the crook of her elbow . . . And she would have done anything he'd asked.

They kiss again in the crowded room, oblivious and modern in their kiss, then draw apart, separate, and my shocking mother slowly turns from him, she stands with him and looks at the room, at the lights of the room that are in her eyes. Something is wrong with her eyes. She looks around her . . . So many people. My mother could never have guessed there would be so many people she might know. So many people when before, at home, there were no other people. There, it was only her own family she knew, only them behind a high garden wall.

She thinks, this party room is not like home at all.

It is brightly lit here, white and yellow, and the glasses held up in the hands of the party guests twinkle like decorations. Young women stand arranged with men. They wear dresses made of thin stuff that's fashion for the time, swathed and draped around them as if they are made of nothing, and have no bodies, only whiteness beneath the dress which is wrapped one wafty layer around the other, thin swathe over thin swathe until the colour has built up in a soft pale cloud. At the lobes of their ears stars are pinned, points of light. They lay thin cigarettes down into ashtrays when they stand up to dance and their tips in the shallow dish burn.

"Do you know . . . ?"
"Have you met . . . ?"

Young men stand next to the women, as close as they can manage without touching. They are clean and new, with their hair brushed back and damp, their neck-ties knotted, lemon, fuschia, rose, full at their throats as flowers. They can't talk at first, for wanting to please. They wait for the words of the women, listening intently to their stories, then after the fragment of silence that follows, they smile or reply or put back their clean shining heads and laugh.

"But of course, you have to meet them," says one young man.
"He's a piece of heaven," says a girl to another.

"And can he *dance* . . ."

In the midst of this crowd my mother unjoins from someone she's just met. Only for frail minutes at a time can she be without my father now. Already she's too used to him, looks out all the time for his smile, waits for his soothing touch on her, and for his part he still gives her the help she needs.

For now, he will help her with a party. He will be there, behind her or at her side, where she expects him to be. He will have his large hand at the small of her back. He will put his lips to her ear, when she needs it, to whisper: *Comfort, comfort.*

My thin mother wavers on her high pointed shoes, her ankles are such fine bone they might snap. She steps backwards, she turns, steadies herself in the high shoes. Yes, he's there where she knew he would be. If she fell against him he would hold. He moves closer towards her, she to him, weakening to him.

She imagines herself saying, turning to everyone in the room and calling out in a clever voice: *Don't you know, we're mad for each other!*

She hasn't known my father for more than a few weeks but already, with her shoes and thin bones, she is thinking about marrying. She's thinking of living a whole life with him, running out from the house where her own father lives, her red hair flying behind her like a rag. Running out, forever! And never going back. Never going back to her father's house again.

So she moves towards this man and he waits for her, and together they stand quite still, one against the other, kept desire in the way their bodies are bent together. They *are* mad for each other, it's true. My mother has already become an outsider to the crowd of people at the party, they are starting to see her differently now. She's no longer the shy girl with her arms always crossed over her breasts. No longer is she turned towards the corner of rooms, away from strangers' extended hands. Even the brother she knows best doesn't telephone any more, doesn't write the funny letters, the cards with pictures chosen just for her. He stays away from town with his wife.

Something has altered in my mother and he is afraid of it, the brightness in her eye. The quiet look she used to have when she was a girl has gone and the brother doesn't like to see the bright chip of light in her dark pupil now, the quick glances, the darting eyes of addiction. She has become someone he doesn't know and the brother lays the fault full in the lap of the big foreign man. The man with his heavy black hair, and his guttural voice, with his fat, sweet-smelling cigarettes . . . Him.

None of this matters to my mother. She has barely noticed her brother's silence these past weeks. She sees only my father now, every day and night, waking, in dreams. Imagines only him, hears only him.

She has her hand in his, holds him tighter as the evening closes in around them. As time passes, light into dark, smoke curling at the edges of ashtrays, fragments of food eaten away, small car-casses on a silver tray picked clean, this party turns into the next party, and the next, and the next, all other parties are this one, other evenings, all the parties she has ever known spin around in my mother's light head, and she holds tighter to my father's hand, for balance. Nothing else matters to her now but having him, keeping him. She's never had a boy all for herself before and this one is a man. She whispers words about him urgently to herself, at night, before lulling herself into a heavy sleep, whispers to herself about him even now, when he's right by her side.

"I love you. I love you."

"I want you to keep me."

The whisper more like a plea than a command.

"It's you, only you."

"I'm in love with you."

To the rest of the people in the yellow-lit room, my mother is slipping away. She is leaving them.

In the brightness of light and glass and movement, in the midst of the talking, from out of the swirl of dancing, from the music coming down the halls, my father remains quiet. He stands back, it's as if all the workings of him are winched back, held in check for now, as if something very powerful is keeping taut all his strings.

The people in the room can see how different he is from them. He has his own shadow in him, his own dense foreign blood keeping him apart. Like he's been alive for hundreds of years, like he might bleed black. The thick hair on his head is uncombed, it may smell bad. The edges on his jacket are frayed and his inside pockets have holes so he cannot keep his things there – his cigarettes, the jewelled lighter. Instead he must put these things away in the pockets of his trousers, where my mother can feel them when she comes up close.

They're kept in the dark place there, resting by his thick thigh, or in his shirt, or at his belly, tucked under his belt, where he can feel them.

By now he has truly fixed my mother up. She wants him all the time, grabs onto him at every party like a crazy girl, on her shoes, and the other women know there's something going wrong in her by now, not fully developed but already something too much like fever, in her clutching grab, in the working of her fingers against his cuff.

Looking back, I can see the infection beginning in the two of them together, right now I can see it. Here is one night, one party, in a hotel, perhaps, in a drawing-room in someone's house, just one little party but my parents are feeding on it like dogs, my mother's quick tongue moistening her lips. Here she is in her lovely dress, and she's dancing too much, talking too much. She shakes her hair too much down her naked back, the back of her dress is pulled down too much.

All the people in the room who were supposed to be her friends stare, she switches and flicks her red hair. Now, with the strange man beside her whom she loves, she can leave them all. She can be a stranger to them all like her lover is a stranger and then she won't ever notice how his face is different from the others, how his hands, moving amongst other hands for drinks and cigarettes, are huge. She won't have to hear that he speaks to her in a strange way, using his accents with her for glamour, and all his foreign words . . .

With her longing and greed for him she won't notice that she can't understand most of the things he says. She wants to be like him, a stranger, as she has always felt a stranger. Yet he could be telling her anything, he could be cruel to her, or gentle, or he could say the most terrible things about what he's going to do to her and she would not hear it, his few words of English separate from the acts they commit together.

This kind of behaviour my mother knows.

She knows "I love you, I love you," whispering on and on in her head, round and around, and she also feels the prick beneath the words.

"Darling," he says, "I want you, I adore you."

He uses the words to keep her longing for him fresh.

And my poor mother knows the words. She's used to the false smooth surfaces of the words and the quick sharp unspoken thing beneath.

"Look at yourself," my father says, and in the midst of the party he takes her over to a long mirror to see. At their back, the party swarms, grows louder. Other people are talking, flirting and dancing, they are making plans for future meetings . . . But my mother is silent. My father holds her in front of the mirror, he has pulled back the hair that has fallen over her face so her neck is arched back, pulled right back like an animal's neck, so the blue vein beneath the skin jumps.

*

"Look . . . Look . . ."

With one long finger he traces like a line for a cut down the side of her face, presses into the hollow of her throat to stop the pulse. With the other hand he comes up against the inside of her thigh, holding her there, in place, forcing her legs apart, hurting her.

"Look at yourself," he says, and she stands there in front of her image, only feeling him, the hurt of him.

"Can't you see how . . ." he pauses, searching for the word he wants to use, "How beautiful you are?"

And deep in my mother's heart there is a crying sound, because this feeling is too familiar to her. She recognises what her new lover is doing. And though the feeling of needing him is stronger than ever before, "I love you, I love you," whispering harder than before and more urgent, still . . . He pricks her.

She looks into the mirror and for a second it's not him she sees, it's someone she already knows.

How long ago these long nights of my parents' first meetings, the dainty cruelty of early love turning, over days, over weeks, into a fine blade they could cut each other with. What night was it my mother left her family forever, and her friends, ran out of the party into the cool streets with a man she didn't know. They ran down the dark streets together, down empty roads. The trees were loaded with blossom in the spring night and it seemed, to my mother as she looked up, the blossom petals were like thick flakes of salt scattered upon the dark sky; they stung her eyes.

Everything was in that moment then, when she ran out with my father that night. Everything was gathered up for that moment when they ran and ran into the darkness, all for my mother's huge love, and that moment could not last.

"Your father was always too much a stranger to stay," she told me, when I was not old enough to hear about it, not understanding her tears, her naked back open to the night sky.

"I have nothing left of him now but then, when we were together, there was colour, sense. There was the fragrance of cold water, the delicious taste of the cold. Every piece of meat I ate was from the animal, juice from peaches and strawberries ran down my chin, bright red . . ."

"Do you understand?" she said. "The colours? How he made me see through the glass?"

I wanted to move away, but she had trapped me in warm water. In the bath where she had placed me there was nowhere to go.

She leaned in across the warm water and pulled me, closer, closer to her.

Do you understand? You are part of him. You are what I have left of him, your little bones. It's his blood when you cut, his coarse black hair that I hold in wet hanks when I wash you . . ."

And she held me closer and closer, and I could feel her heart jumping in her like a caged thing as she kept me, and wouldn't let me go.

"You have his hair, his eyes . . ." my mother said, and yet for all her urgent touching, I was never a substitute for him. Though the rest is in place, all her stories intact – there his hands with her small hands in them, there his hot breath, her dress ripped through . . . Though I can imagine so much that happened between them, I can't yet see the ending in my mind. I can't yet see . . . Did he quietly close the door when he left, knowing it was for the last time? Did he strike her, argue, make her cry? Put his hand over her mouth so he wouldn't have to hear her? Or kiss her, push his purple tongue deep into her mouth so there couldn't be any words? Did he pack a bag beforehand, fold his shirts, decide which pair of shoes were the best to take? Or did he just leave as he arrived, coming out of his lonely past to be with someone else for a while, then disappearing back into it in the same way, carrying no thing.

All my early years my mother kept on with the stories, all the time we were living in our one room and I came to learn them, know them, listening to them from my place where I stood at the window.

"Now you only have me . . ." her voice was murmuring at my back.

"You will have to believe in me . . ."

In those days the house had a fruit shop on the street level, and the Moroccan ladies bought their fruit there, I could see them, below the window where I stood, in their long printed cotton dresses, with their wrapped heads and their polished skin. They moved in a way that had magic. They brought their tiny babies to the shop, bundled up in a length of bright cotton, and at first when

I saw the babies they were wrapped to their mother's back, but later they were let out of the cloth, and they walked, they ran ahead of their mothers in the street.

All those years I watched. I watched the babies grow, run away. I heard my mother's voice behind me as I watched from my place at the window.

"You have his look exactly," said my mother as the years went on.

She was slowly leaving. The stuff she was using was all through her by then and her eyes were filmy with it, milky.

"You are dark, like he was dark," she told me, even as she was stroking my light hair.

"You have his dark colouring . . ." she used to say, even as I was looking back at her with her pale eyes.

I remember, when I stood at the window, I heard the sounds of the Moroccan women calling out in the open air. They called for okra, for green lemons, but in our room the curtains were closed against the brightness of the day. While my mother dreamed and talked and slept I hid myself behind the curtain so I could look out the window and see.

Oranges spilled in the gutter, the bright fabric of the women's dresses turned and swayed, pink cotton and green silk moving in the light. A thin dog with a tartan collar sniffed a box of spiky vegetables, then lifted his leg and peed a thick yellow stream.

I wanted to go outside, but my mother was sleeping.

"His eyes, his skin . . ." she murmured, shifting, gently falling, in her sleep.

"You could be him . . ."

My face was up against the window. It was so sunny outside. The dog was wearing a tartan collar.

"His eyes, his skin . . ."

I put my hand to the glass, I leaned in. The glass held me.

FIVE

The place where I lived then, a lot of people know it. They are familiar with this part of town, they come here, week-ends mostly, when the market is on, and tourists, lots of tourists love this road. It's not a beautiful street, or wide, but there's a curve to it that plays a clever trick with the eye. You always feel here you could be somewhere else, heading either east or west, the sun setting at queer angles and the slight breeze against your cheek fresh as if it's off some large dark foreign sea.

It's a narrow road, that's part of it, like a pathway sometimes dented with footsteps, and when you walk the road it changes. First you pass the little pastel houses that form a neat strip at the beginning, each polished door a different colour from the last. It's so tidy it's like a village here. Cats sit on low walls in the sunshine. They lift their small white paws to their noses and start washing themselves, not stopping when a stranger stops to admire.

"Sweet kitty."

Their hands go out to touch the soft head.

"Let me take you home."

*

A lot of tourists gather around this end of the road, it is so very picturesque for them they can't help it. Their bright woolly jumpers and all the bags they carry form clumps, cars can't pass them, and even their voices jostling against each other in different languages seem to take up all the spaces in the air. These people are on holiday and happy to be here.

Their plastic bags are open to be ready for the things they will find to buy. They've heard about the art deco lamps and the silver jewellery, and the racks of second-hand ball-dresses stuffed with wads of tissue to give them the shape of a woman. They know, too, about the paintings you can find here sometimes, frames and stretched canvasses stacked together but with newspaper wrapped around as if to protect something precious.

I felt like a tourist myself when I returned. They could remind me what it was like to be a stranger. Through the early autumn when I was out in the streets alone and it was sunset, or it was early in the morning and it was quiet, only the sound of my cheap shoes on the tarmac, it was as if anything could happen. Like a person with an empty bag I was expectant.

That was why, when I found the thing I'd been looking for I was not surprised.

He was a man who had been tall once, who would have been handsome. His hair was black, and she would have liked that, how he wore it around his shoulders like a girl, combed clean back from his head so all the little bones there showed. And he was sitting in the Portuguese café . . . That was the best of all.

*

50

When I was a child I loved going to Fernand's café because it seemed to contain within it the things I wanted to possess, all the sweetness. The dates glazed with honey, the tablets of chocolate, even the bread was stuck with candied peel and raisins . . . Everything was warm and tasting of sugar, it seemed full of promises, all the sweet cakes, it smelled of promises. There was the smell of black coffee and bitter foreign brandies, and of rising yeast and sugar, freshly formed marzipan candies laid out in rows. Such sweet memories were contained for me there, in the tiny glass bowls filled with coloured sugars, in the long-handled spoons for ice creams, for stirring orangeade and mixing heavy strawberry syrup into pitchers of iced water.

"Can I help you, my darling Marianne?"

I remember Fernand asking my mother. She was nervous. She hadn't been out for a long time and her hands were shaking when she went into her purse for money.

"I have some special almond pastilles today. Sweet enough even for you who is already the most sweet . . ."

He used to talk with her gently, and I could see my mother relaxing into his promises, in the same way he gave me sweet words that made me feel pretty, as if sugar was dusted behind my ears.

"There is a man here would like to meet you," he promised me, that day, years later, in the same sweet voice as though no time had passed.

"I don't like him at all," he said. "He is much too old . . ."

"I don't think you should go to him . . ."
"I don't like him at all . . ."

And the promise was like the beginning of one of my mother's stories.

Such grandeur was in that place that morning, such a way to begin. Behind Fernand where he stood, ribbonned in light, was his whole café. All his days were there, the celebrations and festivals, feast days. There were baskets of marzipan fruits for the old ladies, chocolate keys and 21s covered with gold foil for the birthdays of all the Catholic boys. There were chocolate crucifixes covered with jewelled papers, sugar flowers for confirmations and christenings . . . Saint's day cakes with stiffened gold paper crowns, boxes of sweets ties with ribbon . . . There were the brightly coloured cartons of dense flat Christian cakes . . . And in the glass cabinet the wedding cakes my mother always loved the best, tied with bows of white spotted net and set high on silver trays. So many fancies glittered and shone in the bright autumn light, they seemed too beautiful for the morning, for the world. They were entirely fragrant, perfect in their cellophane wrappers. To be seen and to be touched. To be eaten.

I rose from my table and walked across the café, through the light to the corner where a man sat also in light, waiting for me. He stood, he pulled out a chair for me to sit more closely to him.

"How do you do?" he said, and his voice was polite, and he opened his mouth to smile and I saw his row of little yellow teeth.

52

"Forgive me forcing you to join me like this," he said. "But you see, I knew your lovely mother. A long time ago, when she was very young, like you are now, and fresh. Please . . ." He motioned towards the plate of cakes Fernand had set down on the table before me. "Eat . . ."

He spoke to me in a quiet way, his accent thick with Russian or Turkish inflections but American too, and he was demure with me, and quaintly mannered, and his pointed teeth showed whenever he smiled. He wore a black suit and a black scarf wrapped around his thin neck, and there were grey gloves laid out upon the table top, and how easy it seemed to begin, as he rolled a cube of sugar while he spoke gently to me, how easy.

Easy that Fernand's café was the place where he found me, so near the house where my mother and I used to live, and also so near his dark house. Easy that when he brought me there, it took only minutes, seconds, to reach the steep front steps that led up to his heavy door. Seconds for the key to twist in the lock, the hinge to swing in. Minutes, seconds, yet already time had changed for me. It was easy, like in a dream, to go inside. Easy to close my eyes there, to sleep, to stay.

As the autumn of our first meeting lengthened into winter, I didn't go back to the café again. I could only remember what it was like to sit there behind the coloured glass window . . . Fernand had been an old man when I'd seen him but he would stay the same, the marble tables would be the same. It would always be that way. Young women would still bring new babies to him and he would call them

53

"little lady" now, give them lemonade in the long glasses, and never let the mothers pay.

At first the memories stayed with me, bright, like little pieces of glass beads on a string, but in time as I was left in a room at the top of the man's house, and I stayed there, and I stayed, and as more and more the darkness of the house came up around me, the glass faded from my mind, and the iced cakes. In the emptiness of my room the dark air of the house was all around me, it came up like a cape and I drew it closer, to sleep.

"Darling . . ."

That was something my mother used to do. Lie down very quietly in the dark and dream.

"Darling . . ." she whispered in the dark.

By then, not moving.

And then, not making any sound at all.

The Quiet Room at the
Top of the House

I see myself in dreams, the same, but different. A young woman with red hair.

Gradually, as I lie in the bed that's been kept for me, the sky that was dark for so long lightens, opens up slowly to the day – first violet, then pink, lemon . . . All pale colours. Later it will rain. Though it seems at this hour too pale and light for the clouds to bank up, it's a trick to make me believe that the colours will hold, that nothing bad can happen. I think now I like those sad unfolding days more. Days that are blue and bright have no infinity in them, the sky comes down like a lid, it presses up hard against the thick window glass and fixes there, with the light of a cold sun to hold it.

Better for me that it is winter. When it is spring, so much time will have passed, I will be sleeping. The pink petals may be thick like confetti in the gutters, the thin branches of the cherry trees waving at me with tiny new leaves, but inside my eyes will be closed. This winter will have to be my spring.

I could be my mother in a dream of springtime, take off my cardigan and feel the soft air on my open arms. I smell the new turned earth in the air, seeds. I am her, playing alone at the bottom of the garden and her daddy far, far away. She whispers to herself "Even if he calls me, I won't be able to hear . . ." And she runs further down the lawn, past the flowers into green. Like her, I smell the sticky shoots pushing through the crumbling soil, there's the dew caught still inside the unopened tulips, on the stems of daffodils still folded close around their yellow hearts.

As spring becomes summer my mother sees the days as endless, she's left alone in the garden and remembers this time as a time of her father's absence, and therefore a perfect time, and complete, that she will always count as her most happy. The blue sky pales with heat, and at the end of the day long blue shadows stretch up the lawn. Still, she doesn't have to go inside, not yet. Her day will lengthen into a warm evening, three stars, a flower. Going inside is for me to do.

It is where I must stay.

Now I've been in the room at the top of the house such a long time all seasons merge. Sometimes when I wake and the night has been very long, then I can't think of the month, the year. I think I am going in and out of consciousness, something happening to my body to make me go from autumn to spring and back into cold.

On these days of pain I imagine flowers, from my mother's dream it's easy for me to imagine them, cut out of the garden where she played, placed in a vase by the window.

*

These flowers were brought to me . . .

I see a huge bunch of fat creamy-headed narcissi, that winter flower with its cool scent, rinsed and clean for a new season.

They were meant for me . . .

I remember I buried my head in the packet of blooms he gave to me. He was smiling like a lover in a song, the scent of the wet green stalks still on his fingers.

For me . . .

The starched white paper around the flowers rustled. I cradled the bundle in my arms like a new baby, breathed in the clean fragrance of the pale heads.

It must be a new season if I can smell flowers? If I can feel how long it is I have been kept inside the room?

First there was autumn, the leaves stiffening like little brown fans on the black branches of the tree outside my window. Then there was an icy wind blowing out of a black sky; it broke every dry leaf loose, it scattered them like bits of dirty paper along the road. The poor tree was left bare with nothing. Its leaves were trampled, and burnt.

All through the autumn it was a skeleton tapping at the glass.

I want to come in.

It didn't like the winter.

I want to come in, it tapped its black bony finger.

There is an old man with black hair. At the beginning when I had bad dreams he comforted me. He put his arms around me and talked to me softly. It seems like a long time ago and he didn't know me well. He would bend to give me comfort then, on his knees gaining my trust.

I want to come in.

How dark his lips. How white and thin his arms and legs.

Darling, I want to come in.

I didn't like the winter but he put his arms around me and it became so I didn't mind the seasons. What difference whether the days were icy or with warm sun? Snow could fall or grass point through cracks in the pavement. Even the tree could cover itself again with thousands of small green leaves. Like a green kaleidoscope the particles would detach, merge, fall. Shift into light, into shadow.

Some weeks are still and cold and I have to stay in bed most of the time, autumn and winter, then spring comes, and summer. All seasons are the same, in this room so long only the light changes, with the year passing; a finger of sun along the window-sill then an entire wall painted gold.

*

Darling . . .

He used to put his arms around me. His black hair fell on my face.

Darling . . .

It was a long time ago.

Now he leaves me in the morning in the empty room.

I wake, and it is the same room.

There is a bed. A table. A vase of flowers. There are no other marks in this room to show someone has been. No curtains at the window, no coverlet for the sheets. The walls are smooth as eggshell and perfectly white, there are no scars on them, or stains. The polished floorboards of this high room are bare. I sweep them every day and no dust is here.

As light deepens, the flowers at the window come slowly into colour. Their waxy petals deepen into colour, each thick bloom surrounding a thin filament, a stamen. The scent of the flowers in their vase, in the coolness of this clean and private room, is too sweet. A knot of pollen has formed in the untouched part of the bloom and the fragrance has been allowed to gather there uncollected, to ripen. As the sunlight becomes clearer in the room the green stems in the glass vase are separate as wands. The window, lying from this bed and looking out, shows only sky.

I could go to the window and stand there for hours and no one would see me, from the street, men wouldn't see. They would only imagine they looked up and saw a young woman; she wouldn't be me.

Even in clear yellow sunlight, this morning, she wouldn't be me.

I am invisible, perfectly alone, and no one knows what we've done. The pigeons on the window-ledge, softly ruffling their feathers, their seeing eyes like orange beads against the glass . . . They won't carry messages of the things that have passed in this room. There are no witnesses for private acts, not even creatures.

He leaves me in the morning and I hear the front door shut, away down the stairs at the bottom of the house. He pulls the heavy front door closed behind him, then everything is quiet.

Here it is my empty room.

No clock ticks, no metal filament wavers to make seconds. All I have is light, the way light fills the air, deepens, then thins off later to grey. So many hours and days I cannot remember them.

Some days it is so warm that I have to peel the sheets off and let the moisture from my skin evaporate. Through the thick glass of the closed window the heat from the sun bores a wide passage, filling the white room with still heavy air that hangs like a ship's sail, waiting.

All time is lying here and waiting . . . For sun to move across the wall and settle on my bed, for the sheets to change to yellow satin, for day to pass so night will come and the man with black hair will come back to my room again.

I could never have enough of him. Of his hands' touch, long fingers, never enough, of the silk of his tongue . . . When he leaves me in the early morning the turn of the key behind him in the heavy front door is the last thing I hear, then I wait. I sleep.

Below me the house is in darkness.

"Promise me you will never go down into my house! That you will stay in your room!"

But I have seen the things.

"Promise me!"

I have the pictures of them in my mind.

I have gone softly down the shallow stairs. I have gone to the landing, to the floors below. I know about the rooms he keeps locked – the rust came off on my fingers like powder. I know about the empty chandeliers that hang like broken necklaces, and the wires that come out of the walls in hooks.

"Promise me!"

But I have seen.

In darkness, I went down the stairs where the air was cool in the passageways, down the halls. My feet were white on the dark boards, they moved slowly like white slippers.

His house was huge.

On either side of the corridor, doors were shut, locked, some with heavy wood and some with chains. There were entrances closed over with boxes, with broken furniture piled like bonfires. There were passages stopped up, but always more stairs, more long hallways stretching into black.

I went deeper down into his house, further down. I heard air that was my breath in the stillness. I put my hands out and a wall was there, it lay flat against my palms. There were so many stairs and I went down them, and some of them were broken but still I went down them, one by one, each broken wooden stair, and I turned, and I felt a thin railing beside me, I felt it turn with me, and then I was out on a balcony, and there was a long window behind it.

Dark light came through the dirty glass. It showed the pale worn pattern of the carpet, the sad empty squares on the walls where paintings had been. It traced the soft torn hangings at the side of the windows, the frail edges of the sill. In the dark light I saw there was a hallway at the foot of the stairs, and it was long and broad and high.

I remember when he brought me here the first time, I saw the hallway then. That day when he opened the front door and, for a minute that day, sunlight came in and I saw the vast shape of the hall, the high corniced ceiling, the alcoves set back. There was a staircase curving into air, up to a high window . . . For a minute that day I saw it, the walls and floor of the hall pale and grey and velvety with dust in the places hands and feet didn't touch . . .

Then he closed the door behind me, and I heard the click of the little lock.

I remember there were books in the hallway, piled up in towers against the walls, and beautiful chests were there, beside the books, they were thickly carved and some of them were open.

He took me past these things that first day, down the hall. He didn't want me to see. He was kissing me, he was pressed up behind me. He covered my eyes as he pushed me on.

"Not here, not this place . . ."

I felt the smoothness of his tongue, the press of hands.

"Upstairs. There's nothing for us here . . ."

But there was everything.

I saw the books again when I went into the hallway on my own and there were hundreds of them, and they were damaged, lashed together with twine and piled high against the wall and the covers of leather and cloth were torn off and left in pieces on the floor. No scholar could trace them. There were diaries, books of blank paper, queer packs of cards. Some had insects eating them, or the pages were torn out or burnt or they were thick with mould down the narrow spine. Pages scattered loose on the floor and their colours had run, crimson and violet and a thin yellow glue like discharge.

The colours bled and bled.

I saw chests next to the books, and they contained paintings, lifted from their frames and rolled up with a twist of cord pulled so tight it cracked the faces of the madonnas, made the paint peel from the thighs and arms of angels. There were vases, and silver and china, and giant serving dishes, and paper packets of jewellery and bolts of cloth and embroideries with stones stitched into them.

In one crate I saw stuffed animals kept in cages, weasels and cats with whiskers and stiffened muzzles and their pickled remains beside them, intestines like worms in a jar, whites of eyes moony against the laboratory glass. In another there were caskets of bones rinsed in vinegar, and parts of the body used for rites of mourning – a thatch of hair to remind of beauty, teeth for strength, fingernail parings kept in a tiny phial.

One by one I opened the chests, smelled the cedar, clean as if it had been newly cut. I picked books from the pile and split back the bindings so I could see the pages underneath.

He used to tell me stories of the hallway, how all his treasures were there. He told me how his house had been beautiful once, and I wanted to believe him, that there had been ball-rooms behind the locked doors, that the hems of ladies' gowns wore away the fine wool from the carpet on the stairway, that once all the tiny lights had burned in the chandeliers, down the halls.

Now all his dark chests were for storage, he said, for spoils of wars, revolutions, the contents of winter palaces . . . And I wanted to believe him. I wanted to think that there were jewel caskets he'd found floating on the muddy waters of a flood, trunks rescued from long journeys, gold medals in cases that his father had worn. I wanted to believe he kept everything from his life, that in boxes were his school uniforms from his boyhood with the priests, dainty linen plimsolls for tennis parties, how when he was a tiny child he wore lace at his throat, gloves. He said he had packed away his mother's dresses, layered in tissue, and that I could wear them. That there were flat boxes of embroidered jackets, shirts with paper collars, fabric bags containing socks, scented lace handkerchiefs . . .

He talked and talked to me then, in my high room.

He stroked my hair.

He told me of beautiful food left over from love affairs, somewhere in one box pickles and caviares, tins of fish with their eyes in, so fresh that when you opened them up they would taste as if you had just taken them from the Black Sea.

He said he could keep me inside and feed me on these foods and no one outside would never know we were here.

"We would be with each other, alone," he said. "Gorging ourselves on fish eggs and champagne . . ." I remember the sound of his voice coming out of the darkness.

Light from the street came through the window and showed his thin hands, his long naked arms.

"We would have preserved fruits and delicious soft rotted cheese, and packets of black chocolate to make you plump . . ."

His thin hands stroked my hair, my face.

"And I would feed you here, in your little room. I would come to you with my knife and my cracked plate. And you will never leave me. You will never leave your little room at all . . ."

Now I have done what he said.

So much time has passed and now I never leave my room for food, or any reason.

Now I am beginning to believe I have never lived anywhere else but here, and sometimes he brings me flowers to the room. And sometimes he doesn't come to see me, and other times he comes at night and then he goes away. Then dawn comes, and for a while it is light again.

I don't go downstairs any more.

The walls there were painted some dark shade of brown, or deepest crimson made dirty with age, with lack of cleaning. I used to know that colour, I think, but with the darkness creeping in, darker and darker as winter comes, I don't know it.

It seems a long time since I have been down in the hallway with the boxes, to smell the contents, to look through his books, his piles of old shirts. A long time since I put my hands amongst the wooden boxes of old silver knives, felt the rims of fine china plate under my thumb, the soft raised bands of gold.

It is as if I have eaten something from one of his tins to make me so forgetful of my old life. As if I have the antique metal of his fork in my mouth to stop my tongue, my lips pressed into one of the sharp deep spoons. It is as if I am already dressed in the antique clothes, wrapped damp stoles around my body, stepped into the same naked silken underwear his mother once wore.

Now I lie in my safe bed, I wait.

I wait and first there is light, dawn's pale colour. Then heat is in the room, then later dusk, and then at last it is night and then he comes again.

He knew by now it would become this way. He knew that he would take me stepping out on the streets, that he would have me slipping into bars. That he would split open stale bags of crisps with his long fingernails, and we would drink whiskey then, or little tumblers of gin . . . And he knew that it would change. There was a bottle of purple wine between us at the restaurant, the shared bleeding steak. The chocolates he brought for me, small gifts like handkerchiefs, silk roses . . . Then these gifts stopped. Our life became closer, closer together, and I no longer went outside in the streets, where people were.

I can't remember if I missed this change, if I was frightened by it – the way the food stopped, the clean clothes. The way the smells became different, no longer the smell of cold air on the streets, or the smell of cigarette smoke in a bar, or the restaurant kitchens . . .

Now everything is inside, the closed-off air, the bed and all I can smell is him – the sweet lime smell he leaves behind him when he's gone. That is the smell at my face now, not flowers. It's the smell of the scent he wears, the sour cut of that odour all through the room, on this pillow. I smell it in private, when I'm completely alone, sweet and citrus in the room, the only smell, the smell of him, like dying. When I lie very still, with the sweet rotted scent he leaves behind him in the room to breathe . . . This is what dying is like. There is no new season, no rinsed green stems in a jar. Only stillness of body, mouth . . . And this close smell.

I have it with me now as light fills the room. As time passes, the way sunlight may fill the lining of an old silk curtain in a far-off bedroom, the way light may fill and bloom behind the rose-coloured silk then fade, shading off into darkness . . .

This is what dying is like . . .

. . . A mother's face, a pale moon, the scent off her cool neck is limes, and off her cheek, off her ripe mouth . . .

This is what dying is like, not a lonely thing, or sad. It comes like velvet. To lie gently here alone, sleep at my back, at my side, at my mouth, dark sleep, and very soft . . .

It is what dying is like.

There is no escape from this.

All over my body I can feel the parts of tenderness, beneath the thin sheeting, I can listen to the sounds of each small wound's pulsing heart. I don't want to see. There is a beating of blood beneath the surface and the beating goes on, on, but no one can see. The darkness covers, it accepts my shape, the hollow at the back of my yellow neck, the long fishbone of my spine. It comes up around me, gently, gently like capes the soft black, and now I am in covers, in wrappings and sleep can take me . . .

The house is silent, the house is as velvety dark, everything powdered and dusted and deep in sleep. I won't hear the sounds from outside, through the thick slab of window glass, I won't hear people. I drift to sleep, in dark I meet sleep, for so long now I sleep, and everything is gentle now, in sleep, and I sleep and sleep . . .

Then, something.

In the darkness, I hear it. A splinter.

A tiny hole of light in the gorgeous velvet dark.

A dot of light, I hear it in the rich fabric, then another, and another.

Letting splinters of light in, not in here, not in this room, not inside my own head.

Drip, drip.

In the dark, pin-pricks of sound but getting bigger.

Drip, drip.

From somewhere far away, far away from me.

Drip, drip.

In the bathroom. It's the slow dripping of a tap I can hear.

*

In his bathroom where he applies his scent, bathes. Runs the thick citrus oil through his hair, down through his body.

Drip, drip.

I can hear each bead of water emerging from the tap, a tiny silver soldier, holding for a second then falling to death on the white porcelain below. Drying to air like he never existed, little man, little bead.

Drip, drip.

Each droplet of water hanging at the lip of the rusted chrome, hanging for one second, two, perhaps three seconds then falling, drip, against the cold white side.

Drip.

Drip, drip.

Drip.

Long seconds pass. What else can I do, only lie here, but the velvet is lifting, the light has come through and made it into shreds, then tiny pieces, light everywhere and now the darkness has gone and the bed is warm but slowly, piece by piece, I wake from the sheets.

I feel my limbs start to come alive, my breath in the air. The sun has moved across the wall and it is twilight. I start to come awake at night.

There is a sound, there is a dripping tap I can hear in the bathroom . . . And I start to come awake, slowly pull back the sheet, like peeling back the cover of sleep, and as I do, there is the huge weight of responsibility for my limbs, to raise them from the bed. I stand up, for a second in the violet twilight there is the shock of my nakedness, then I am upright, not shaking, the dizziness clears.

The floor is far away.

It's down there, far away, miles away. I put one leg in front of the other, take another step and another. The rumpled bed is an island at my back, the sheets are tumbling, but as I walk further it recedes into distance, shrinks to a little iron thing left in the corner of the room.

Outside there is the empty sound of the market packing up.

Old women gather up armfuls of used clothes and bundle them into bin-bags. No one will ever wear them. In the mews, ponies with old bitten hides stand with their heads down in the violet light. Soon the men will come, hook up their heavy carts to the wooden shafts and the small horses will pull them along the darkening streets, going home. The air will thicken like wet ink poured into dry, and in the inky black there will be squares of yellow light, and people behind the yellow squares, standing closely together at a bar or at a table. Their elbows touch.

It comes in a rush, the warmth of being indoors in a yellow-lit place, and it helps me walk, steer a path through the door, across the deep treacherous floor, to the bathroom sly as a thief because I am not supposed to be here.

In this room where he keeps his creams and his scent and his dye . . . In this room where he undresses his old body, lets himself be naked in front of the mirror, and he looks at himself, shaves himself.

He washes the black from his hair here, and it is where he stands, tenderly undoing the damp bandages he wears for his vanity, unwinding them from his raw parts, soothing himself with water . . .

"*Grishtok*, shit . . ."

. . . This is where I hear him spit in the morning, curse. He cleans out his mouth here, swallows, wipes his make-up off and applies fresh brown cream to his face. He comes up close to the vanity glass, draws on new lips, thin black rims around his eyes . . .

I shouldn't be here.

The dark is too close, with the tub crouched on claws, with the mirror cracked . . . It's not safe.

Promise me!"

But haven't I been into his house before?

"Promise me!"

Haven't I seen all the things there are to see?

I sluice the dark watery remains from the insides of the bathtub and I take a cloth to the sides where he has been lying. His make-up has left a skim, and I have to rub hard to remove it, and the flecks of skin, and hair strands, and the dirt . . . But as I wipe down the bath completely, removing the final traces of these stains, the smell of him rises up at me as limes, the scent of his oil that he always wears, on his face, in his hands and hair.

I pick up the cloth and the smell is fresh on it, as if he is there in the room with me, in that moment, the smell of him on my hands.

I place the rubber ring against the plughole, and I can hear my heart beat as I do it. Carefully I press down the plug so it will cover the black scented wad of hair left stranded in the tub, hold it down so it will stay, and the smell is still there, the thin citrus smell that will never go away. I imagine him stroking the lime oil into his face, rubbing it deep into the dry skin, into the creases of his body. I see him combing it through his hair until it is slick, shining like a young man's shining head.

I turn on both taps and let the water come fill the huge bath, to be away from the smell, to be clean, to be clean. Only to lie in warm water, to turn on all the taps and let the water run so the sound of clean water fills the top floor of the house like rivers falling . . .

Yet even as the water runs, scalding and ice cold, even as water pools over the rusty stain at the base of the bath that reminds me of blood, as inch by inch the water rises, dark in the dark air, rising, still the smell of limes is strong. In the water, in the steaming air. Stronger every minute, and sweeter, and the country where he came from seems very close, in the dark scented air . . . The country where old men with painted faces were born, where they were made, with their red lips, with their bright black eyes.

"Promise me!"

Yet the last time when I left my bed and went downstairs to the boxes in the hall . . . I was not frightened.

Though I had touched all his fur coats, all the slippery linings of his jackets he kept in the hall, though I'd seen the old dresses wrapped in tissue, the pouches containing jewellery and pins . . . I was not frightened. I had sat by the boxes in the hall before, I had been through them for food, I had opened up the wooden lids for curiosity and for hunger . . . And even when I had tried on the satin shoes and pumps stitched with beads, opened drawers containing handkerchiefs, valentines . . . Even then, my breath was not tight in my heart as it is tight now when I imagine his face reflected in the mirror.

When I saw his most forbidden books, that last time I went downstairs, it was dark when he came back to the house, and all his books were scattered in the hall, stacked in piles that had fallen . . . So how could he ever know that I had been there? That day, in the dim grey light of the hallway, I went through so many books, in French, Italian and English, unfolding folios of thick card with prints of churches and palaces, of formal gardens laid out and the seeds they could be made from. There were tied envelopes, and I broke them open, they contained fragments of paintings in the Prado or the Louvre. There were damaged reproductions that may once have been part of a game: The leg from the *Maya* hinged in four places, the eyes of the *Mona Lisa* cut out to wear like a mask. I picked it up and placed it against my face. How could he ever know?

The first books were easy. I smiled at some of them. It was the next set of books that were more difficult to see. In these there was no hand of Velázquez, to be cut from his self-portrait and used as a glove. These were anatomies, diagrams of male and female bodies, not cross-sections of a flower. The bones were drawn on white paper, only the kidneys and offal painted in shiny colour. In their detail every fibre in the gland showed itself, the wrap of sinew and vein. They were the bodies of men and women drawn, showing where age and sex could change them, how the slow eating of disease could transform the skin. In some pictures the bones and veins were pulled back to show the tiny sacs deep in the interior, filled with reproductive material that was ready to be burst open and smeared.

There were lopped-off limbs, and joints split open. There were calves and thighs slit down the middle with the insides pinned to the edge of the page, all the muscles and ligaments twisted together and held back with pins. Another book showed the run of blood, from the brain to groin, beneath all the black wiry hairs, and inside the breasts, behind a cage of bone, the great red plane of the heart.

There were heads on top of these dismembered figures, faces. The women had pink cheeks and blonde hair, though their wombs were carved wide open to show the curled foetus growing inside them, their teeth showed in a smile. The illustrator had fallen in love with them a little, he had married them to each other, given the wife a set of earrings, the castrated man a wedding band.

Volume after volume I saw, and, though the covers were off and many pages were glued together or burnt, still I couldn't stop, I kept looking for the next volume, then the next, and the next. There were pictures of victims who seemed pulled out live for dissection, or were half decomposed, bodies too soft for a scalpel, from graves, women screaming in child-birth as the knife went in, the long pin.

The dust and dead moths were thick in these books . . . It was as if no one had opened them for hundreds of years. I should not have opened them, but by then I was prepared enough by blood and hearts, so when the other pictures came, the bodies strung up on racks, and pinned against the wall, they seemed no worse than the rest . . .

Now darkness gathers in the dark room, with heat and steam, and as the water rises and his smell, with the sweet and filthy odour in the cloth, in my nose, at the back of my throat to taste . . . I feel him too close for it to be day. The shuttered room lets in only thin rods of light, darkest gold, like bronze and the bronze rods are deepening into twilight now, it gets darker.

I lower myself into his huge rusted tub, into his water . . . and his smell is everywhere. In the mirror, as I let myself go gently down, I see my white face, burnt fever eyes, my body bright as a piece of paper underwater. It is me here, in the stink of piss and blood and citrus on the tile, against the porcelain side of the tub, in the mirror, in the water, me.

That day when I took up the last of his books, I knew I would not go downstairs again. The heavy cover, inside the outer wrapping showed writing I'd never seen before, engraved deep into the leather, black grooves into black like scratches from claws. There was the creak and split of the spine, then the volume yielded to me, though it was not meant to be opened, it opened. The endpapers were yellow, marked with the trail of serpents that snaked from one side of the inside cover to the other. Stuff came out of their tails, mucus, eggs, and they joined, in the centre of the book the serpents met, entwined around a woman finely drawn as a spider-leg in ink. She was cut in half where the pages rose up, one half of her on the inside front cover, the other half on the back. Snakes grew inside her. Her head was back and a long tongue curled from her open mouth. Her black eyes were wide open and staring as bullets.

The pages were dry but I turned them, all drawings in the black spider ink, all bodies. One figure was strapped to a wheel so her legs were open and something came out from between them. There was no face, no hands. Other bodies were trussed and bound as though they were to be cooked and eaten, the ankles corded to the wrists, a leather gag around a woman's mouth so blood ran down her chin like gravy. There were men and women dressed in strange outfits, a child soldier in a uniform tightly buttoned back to front, men dressed in ball-gowns with their groins tightly swaddled, women with nail-studded breastplates, spikes holding them in place through their legs. There were pictures of whips, cords, page after page of flayed skin, long pelts of flesh revealed where the leather had taken the skin clean off, and there were burnings, with boiling water and flame, and the skin had cooked and crackled like glaze.

Still I turned the pages. There were books that showed hanging chains, clamps, masks of silk. There were ankle bindings and wrist braces, and pictures of women who had been marked by these devices, whose breasts and thighs were cut and bruised, while their eyes were bandaged. In one picture I saw an instrument so fine I would never have thought it could be used on someone still alive, the fine steel with a tiny barb on the end, a hook that the woman might not even feel until it was deep inside her and when withdrawn, would have her bleed and bleed at a touch, like a little girl.

I turned the pages, all I wanted, to look and look . . . A boy laid out as if dead on a block, a girl with a single thread of blood running down the centre of her white body, where she'd been cut neatly for a seam . . . There were her parted lips, her palms held upwards to catch the light, the cut in skin marked as a dress-maker's line of stitching, and I was not frightened then. I wanted to look. I loved her, the poor dead woman, I wanted to be that way.

The bathroom is cool now, the water warmer than blood temperature. Day seems far away. The water is dark, licking the side of the tub, licking it with little dark tongues then stilling, trembling around my body and settling in a darkened film. In my mind as I lie here only breathing I hear my mother's murmuring voice, her soft insane voice murmuring in my ear as she wet me.

"Your Daddy left me your little body to hold . . ."

Murmuring, not like words, like something already in my own mind.

"Your little body . . . It belongs to me."

I close my eyes to forget, to close away the words in the warm water, and the memories, and her lipstick stains on my skin. I want to forget it all in warm water, only smell the oil, only think about thin white arms reaching out of the water to wrap around me. All I want is to be covered by water, in disguise, covered in water to my neck, dressed completely in the dark lapping, quietly, quietly. I keep my eyes closed to continue the dream of him, only him, no mother, no father. To be prepared, made perfect for him, only him, to disappear in him.

When the darkness is complete I open my eyes.

The water is cold. I am numb, nothing left. I rise from the cold water, take the towel from the back of the door and uncover the belt that is hanging there.

The bronze rods of light have faded, the shutters' gaps are dark, but I don't know how late it is. All I see is the belt curving, darker than the darkness, a long thick black strip lengthening from the hook, touching the floor, just the tip of it, like the tip of a black tongue touching.

Like silk darkness touching . . . On my lips and skin, in the strands of my hair. I feel the smoothness of the polished end of leather smooth like the smoothness of silk on skin, the smooth edges on my skin of the tiny knives that hang from the belt, their blades thin enough for butter.

There's the weight of the leather, it hangs motionless from the hook beside me. I reach for it, I pull it and it falls down easily into my lap.

I don't hear his key turn in the door downstairs.

※

I touch the blades, the tip, the buckle, I feel the loveliness of the heavy coil resting in my lap, and I don't hear him approach, softly, in the dark stairway, coming closer. As I trace the edge of the leather, I don't hear him.

I look up.

He is standing at the doorway.

He is smiling.

A Dark Red Light

ONE

My mother was beautiful. To call her beautiful is an act of worship, I know, and that is a difficult thing. Beautiful is a word you have to choose carefully, yet still I felt it, when I was a child. I still feel it, I still feel about her that difficult word.

As she lay on her sofa in our dark room she was like a stem and flower, a delicate and tended bloom. The pale thin skin of her had to be kept cool during the day. She had to be kept indoors, away from the light, and alone, with no loud noises, no smell, nothing to touch her if she didn't want it.

When I was very young, I watched over my mother, at four or five I began doing it, I began to learn the responsibility of taking care of her then.

I stood by the sofa while she slept, or I quietly played. Or I stood at the window, behind the curtain looking out so the yellow sun wouldn't come in. I was learning to watch, to look over someone who is loved, but at the same time I was learning to see other people, out in the street, to see how they behaved – learning how it would be for me when I stepped outside.

There was a girl leaning into a boy's neck, a woman carrying flowers. There was a man, with tins of food in a plastic bag. He lived in a doorway over the street and I saw him there, saw how, when he needed to eat, he took the things out of the bag and arranged them, using a knife to get into the tins. I saw many lonely people like him, the forkfuls of greasy food held up to their mouths, the way some people who had no home disappeared into an alley or a doorway. The way all of them quickly turned away their eyes.

If any of those people had lifted their heads, if they had looked up . . . They would have seen a child, perhaps four years old, or five, or six. She would have been watching them. They would have seen me.

It seemed when I was small I was always at the window. Looking out at the day while my mother slept on the sofa, later, standing there in the dark, and as the years passed I became taller at the window, I could see further down the street. At first it was only my chin resting on the sill, looking up at me then you would have only seen the top of my head, one pair of watching eyes. But as I became older and I didn't need the box to stand on, I could stand with my fingertips touching the sill and by then I was ten years old, and eleven, and everything that happened to me then, in my eleventh year was expected. I'd been watching for it at the window, in our dark room. I'd been waiting for it.

Mother, I still hear you in the sirens.

*

Even now, I hear you, and I see you in the flashing of red on our dark wall.

On–off. On–off.

I see the red light complicated by the black that flicks into it with every second.

On–off. On–off.

On our dark wall.

The red and black like danger lights for ships that have gone too far out to sea, like for murder, like for late-night drinking bars, and you. Mother, I see you in the dark light, the red flashing before my eyes . . .

On–off. On–off.

Your lovely body lain out, your legs and arms I arranged all in a piece so you could lie quietly there, but still I hear you in the screams of the ambulance outside. I see you reflected in the red eye of its flashing light, in the red and dark light in our sad room, in the lights of police cars, hospitals. Mother, darling, I see you, down through the dark corridor of all the years – I see you. Your slow smile when you picked me up in your arms, your smiling red lips behind the swing of your heavy dark-red hair. Your long fingers playing with mine, interlacing like weaving, your slow undressing of me.

There was the way you sat on the side of the tub while I bathed, smoking white cigarettes with bright tips that glowed in the dark, and sometimes you lit candles for me off the end of your cigarettes, as I lay in the warm water in the dark, and when the flame caught the wick I saw your eyes for a second reflect the tiny fire.

Mother, I believe you cared for me and perhaps, I don't know, it was love. The pills you took, all the bottles lined up on the little table, the silver tray with the drugs you used, the needles and the cotton . . . I know you tried with me, to be well. I believe it. You picked me up in your arms.

I was the one who called the men you needed, and they always came.

There was the doctor. The man for the hospital. The man for the pills and bags of china powder.

All the numbers I needed to call were written on the wall by the telephone out on the landing.

"Call him now, honey. Tell him I need him to come right now . . ."

The hallway out on the landing was papered with roses, I remember, with the numbers and names written around them. They were big dark-pink cabbagy roses with no thorns, only vines and leaves twisting up the wall to hold their heavy heads, and the writing of numbers and names went all around them, like swards of tiny moths and flies. The wallpaper was badly stained too, in parts, with yellow from cigarette smoke, and damp coming down in thick lines from the high ceiling, and the plaster showing in places where the paper had come away, like the white skin on a woman's legs showing from a cut in a dirty dress.

I remember the landing as though I'm standing there now. The grey smell coming up from the carpet. The pale filtered yellow light through the dirty glass over the front door reaching up the first flight of stairs to the landing, touching me, where I stood by the black telephone, patterning me in and out of dirty yellow light and in shadow.

I remember how the telephone numbers were written in pencil, in my mother's miniature handwriting, writing that was too delicate for prescriptions, or for writing to a family to ask for money, too minute to live anywhere except in the numbers written between the roses, the name and the number fitted in between a vine and a leaf and a huge flowering head. I was young when I made the calls first – I had to stand on the chair to be able to read the numbers – but later, as I grew taller, it was easy to stand right next to the black phone, feed the coins in and dial, talk to anyone my mother needed.

Make the call for me, honey.

There was the man who kept the bottle store, who delivered the heavy box himself and kept credit for us because sometimes my mother would sleep with him. There was the cigarettes boy, and the man who sold bandages.

There were men from the hospital, but most important of all was her favourite doctor whose name was not on the medical list and who let me phone him to order the drugs she used, when she could not speak. Sometimes he came directly to our room, after I had ordered, even if it was late at night he came straight to our house and I let him in the front door. He came up to our room and from

89

the beginning he took charge of the things my mother needed.

He prepared her thin arm by wiping it with disinfectant, he unwrapped the little package that contained the new syringe, and he held the binding around her arm so the needle would go right in to the soft part, where the blood was. As my mother's body took the clear stuff in, he pushed the syringe down and further into the soft part, further until it was empty, and she arched towards him.

Then we knew it was done, he and I, when she made that delicate spasm, and I saw her relax, her eyes go over, and her slow smile for the doctor, as he leaned in towards her.

That was the time when I went into the bathroom to play, I always played then because I knew I couldn't be there with them any more, even though I thought they probably wouldn't notice me, still, it was easy to go into the bathroom. I talked and sang so I couldn't hear them, and I lay in the empty bath with all my toys, stroking their hair and fur, and sometimes practising that silent arc my mother's body had made, the way her back and shoulders had lifted and stilled . . . Sometimes I played to be that silent acrobat too.

All the men that visited her in our room didn't change our lives, I knew that as I lay in the empty bath on my own.

It didn't mean my mother didn't miss my father all the time, think about him, and remember me. She simply needed the other men, with the things they brought her, pills and bourbon and cigarettes. Since my father left she'd needed them. Besides, the men were clean, with nicely combed hair, and some of them kept sweeties in their pockets for me. None of them were my father so we were safe. My mother's loyalty could remain sealed, kept perfect, because none of the men coming into her were him.

Her favourite thing to say was that she'd been given the kind of marriage too fine to last.

Every day, she said, my father made such gestures to her, the way he kissed her it was as if it was the first time. Every night there was fresh bedlinen, he took care with the little hooks and openings in her clothes, the row of buttons at her back. For this reason, everything so perfect, they never had to find out who the other was. For all the gay parties, my mother's expensive dresses, for all the crystal flutes of cold champagne, she never knew anything about the man she married, and he believed she was a rich girl who would not damage, when really, she was more broken inside her white party dress than he would ever know.

In the end all that happened was he made her more lonely, more strange.

The habits that had started early in her life, the only daughter in a houseful of boys who learned in the nursery not to talk, not to speak out against men . . . These habits came to rest in my father, after him she would never change. Her brothers used to play with her like a baby, like a little doll, and her mother, from the beginning, had always been someone who was sick, so quiet in a bedroom somewhere in the house that when she died my mother never missed her, she never cried in the night.

For her, it was as if there had never been a family.

The brothers were sent away to school, university, then on to jobs and marriage and careers abroad, and my mother grew up alone in her father's big house; she was used to the silence of the walls. She was familiar too, with her remaining parent, his mouth in a line as he sat with her at the dining-room table, both of them eating the cold bland food that had been prepared on his instruction. That kind of food suited him, he kept his head down as he ate. When he gave my mother a wallet of money to buy dresses, he also looked away, like he was paying her.

Perhaps she looked too much like his wife, and that's why he could not hold her eye, thinking she would get sick, too, and die, if he loved her. Or perhaps he had no love in him to show with his eyes. Who was to know . . . Except that when my mother's hand lingered too long upon his sleeve, when she was asking him something, or wanting forgiveness, he hated it, and he shook her hand away. And if her kiss goodnight was too moist or cool or girlish, or there was the mark left on his cheek from her new lipstick, then when he went to bed that night there were tears in his eyes from the feelings she had given him, disgust and rage, desire, still there from the moment when his daughter had approached him.

This was my poor mother's life by then, when she was so young.

Yet, the first dance she attended, the year her father had given her the money for dresses, I imagine how my beautiful mother would have been. So silent and new in her life.

Her first dance . . . And I imagine how it would have been . . .

Two

You can smell powder drifting in the air. Late afternoon and the sun is golden around her head as she sits at her dressing-table before the oval mirror, fingers straying through her hair, pinning it, curling it in strands to make the ends tendril and fall. The long curtains at the open window drift and bloom in the golden light; there is the sound of evening birdsong, the movement of leaves in the warm, late-summer breeze, the thinness of leaves yellow-green with the light through them, shifting against each other, touching.

Tonight, when the light is golden, there are so many ways for my mother to make herself beautiful. She is seventeen years old.

She lifts a skein of hair from the back of her nape and feels the weight of it in her hand, the softness of her hair, and the colour is bright and coppery and full of light.

"All my life . . ." She murmurs to herself as she plays with her hair, pinning it this way, and this way. Twisting it now into a shining chignon, feeling the soft weight of it in the white hollow of her neck where the sun never gets to, now undoing that shape so it drops free, making a new plait, tying it, putting it into a fat roll, catching a side of hair and bringing it up . . . Her hair forming the patterns of all the women she can be, tonight if she chooses, or perhaps for all her life, be someone else entirely, whoever she decides she wants to be.

Her face, you would not say is pretty, or like a girl. You may not say at first it is beautiful but my mother is very beautiful. Her light eyes have flecks of gold in them, reflecting, they make her skin seem more smooth, make the bones beneath her skin model her fine face like forms in wax. The pupils of her eyes are dilated from looking at herself, as she takes her hair and smooths it back, not even leaving one strand strayed, all of her hair smoothed back so you can see her entire face exposed, the planes of her cheeks and forehead rosy and tan from the sun, now polished by the late-afternoon light into a dark gleam.

All summer she has been at the cottage with her father, sailing away from him in her own small boat.

She has been sailing away every day, far enough away that she can get to her private rock that comes out of the water and has a ledge carved in it flat and long like a bed, a hidden place where she can go. She has been anchoring her boat there and undressing in the wide blue air, sunning herself naked in the cleft of rock where he can't get to, where he could never see. All summer her face has been a lamp, at the tennis parties and drinks parties on long flat lawns blue with shadows, all summer her face has glowed with sunshine, and her teeth have showed white in a smile whenever she has dared to smile, a frightening smile for the young boys maybe, the way she shows all her white teeth in her tanned face, but exciting too, for those of them that dare come up close to her with their hair still damp from swimming.

They were never able to have her.

All summer my mother has been alone with her father at the cottage. They have been together on their own, not even the housekeeper comes with them in summer. No one comes, there are no visitors.

In the early evening the man takes the tray of drinks and sets it down on the table under the big oak, and the girl, his daughter, will come out at the appointed hour and stand with him there, beneath the big tree. That is the routine every day; they meet each other there. To the man, it seems the girl floats towards him when she comes, floating across the blue lawn in her white dress. In the dusk she blooms like a flower, her light skirts are petal. The father notices this, notices how the light plays around her thin arms, how her waist is so small a man could encircle it with his hands, knows how big those hands would be upon her. And all summer my mother has stood quietly, when her father mixes up her first drink for her, and her second.

Like a young boy he goes through his routine with her, shy in parts, then bold, telling her about this drink or the other, how strong the drinks are, showing off to her . . .

And all the time my mother is feeling the presence of this handsome man with his dark-grey hair cut close to his head, his dark profile in the remaining light, feels him next to her as the man who has fathered her, once held her in blankets awkwardly in his arms, passed her back to his wife for milk. This was the man who scolded her, sent her to school, once cleaned up the mess when she was sick. He was the man who saw her all the years when she did not see herself, before mirrors, before she learned to smile at her reflection in order to receive back her own smile, before other people, before other eyes went out for her, he was the man who, at night in his dressing-gown, would leave his room to walk down the hall and come into the room of his baby daughter, his only daughter, to stand there, for a long time, just watching her, thinking about her.

This is the first year my mother's brothers have not come to the cottage for the summer. The first time they have not left their wives and children and their jobs in the city or abroad to come. There were three brothers, but my mother always saw them as one, all boys together, always at the cottage playing together without her but still, it was safer when they were there. Though in the past she has felt the difference – the girl swimsuit hanging outside on the line to dry – and in more recent years when undressing at night, with the dress lain out on the bed, and the unclipped bra, lace shorts . . . It was better then, when the boys were there at the cottage, calling out to each other across the lawn, telling jokes to their father.

Now that it's just him here with her it is too quiet, her girl's voice is too soft in the night air.

Nevertheless, for this reason, her seventeenth year, it is the first year when she can go out alone at night. She is old enough. Until late at night her father can pace the house, returning over and over to the decanter of whiskey on the sideboard. He can walk to every window of the cottage and look out across the sea-grass lawn, across the hedge, down the fields to the sea. He can keep all the windows open to the night air, to the sighing sound of the sea missing her, everything is missing her. He might keep all the lights turned on waiting for her to come home, every lamp and wall light, every bedside candle light, even in the empty rooms, and he can stand in all this forced light and burn for his daughter to return home early, earlier, to try and pretend to himself that she never left. She is of the age now when, if she chooses, she may never return.

He knows this, but still the lights burn, still he paces the house in the brightness, feels the heat of his waiting break out the door into the dark open air, so he's pacing about the dry garden at night, waiting, waiting.

My mother does always come home to him.

Night after relentless night, all through the long summer, she comes home, perhaps in the car of one of the damp-haired boys, yet though her powder may be on him, a dust of white on his dark jacket, she is always apart from the boy. Her father watches the car's headlights come up the road, the headlights passing along the top of the hedge, swinging inwards at the gate, coming up the sandy drive. Inside the cottage he stands shock still, waiting, listening, or outside in the garden he stands still and alert to the movements of the boy. But no matter what he imagines he hears, or what he imagines he sees, he cannot say a word. He cannot stop the boy's light kiss, come between his lips and his daughter's lips, change her growth, stop time. He cannot rage in a room full of seconds while minutes tick by, turn into days then years. He cannot stop the future opening for my mother. He thinks her mouth this minute is becoming soft, her lips parting, her hands may be reaching out, but there is nothing he can do. He hears, in the sea's moan, sad wash against the shore, all the things he cannot bear to hear. All the father has are seconds to share with her, in his room of seconds.

All he can have is a thin sliver of time with her, a fraction, in the garden, in her white dress.

"Grasshopper, Sea Breeze, Old-Fashioned . . ."

In the early evenings on the lawn he tells her his list of special drinks, wanting to make them for her, wanting to show her how things can be done.

"These young fellows, they don't know how to mix a drink. They couldn't make you what you wanted . . ."

He has turned to the table set out under the tree, with the tray of bottles upon it, but he can't see what's there.

"These young fellows . . ."

He looks but he can't see.

He never guesses that my mother has no lover, doesn't even know how to talk to a boy, that she has barely any time left for herself after him, that he has it all, that he can have it, she's used to it that way. Blindly, he takes bottles from the tray, aware of her standing beside him, aware of her beside the blue tree . . . He can hear her breath. In a rush, he mixes the drinks, he pours them from the silver shaker, from the glass martini jar. He swivels ice around in the punch jug, stirs the clear contents of a tall pitcher, skewers fruit with a fork, bites the olive hard.

"You know, I used to have the reputation of being able to fix one of the best cocktails around. What do you think of that?"

By now, there have been lots of drinks, so when my mother looks up from her seat by the tall tree, up into his eyes to answer, she cannot bear it. All of his thin life is there, in his eyes, it's all on show for her.

As soon as she can, after he has handed another triangle of glass to her, and after she has taken it from him, felt the touch of daughter to father in their fingertips meeting at the thin rim of the glass, then she will drink this cocktail, and another, if he wishes, as he will, she knows, and then, kissing him lightly, her lips just a touch upon his hard cheek, then she will slip away, finally, she will slip from under the tight arms that try and hold her, will run from those eyes, from him, though he would never do anything to her now, out here, in the garden, when there is still some light in the sky for him to see his own hands and what they are doing.

So for now she will take the drink, and finish it. Then she will run away.

These are her thoughts as she sits at her dressing-table in late summer, that same summer of her seventeenth year. She thinks the thoughts, but without words, as if in a dream. She's back in town now, the cottage by the sea is locked up, and it will be autumn soon.

"All my life . . ."

My mother murmurs words, sentences that have no ending. Somewhere, in the big house, in one of the rooms, is her father.

"To lift up into the air and dream . . ."

Finally, with pins and a brooch, she has made the shape for her hair that she wants.

She turns sideways to the mirror to see, her long golden neck, her red hair caught up by the silver ornament. She sees the line of her shoulder in the mirror, and the tiny bone that juts out above the outline of her shoulder, and all her skin is gleaming from her bath, buffed in the remaining light into gold. My mother rises from her chair before the round mirror, dressed in underthings, frail pieces I can barely see on her, yet she rises, dressed only in these things. Here in her room, in this light, nobody can spy on her. She can be alone with herself if she wants, she can stand here, or over by the long mirror, she can be in her own bedroom dressed only in these tiny things, and no one will see, and she can dream. She can feel hands going down the length of her long body, or she can hold herself in her own arms, or unfasten the tiny buttons of her clothes, step out of them and be completely alone with herself.

Tonight though, she has no time for the dreaming games, instead she must think out into the night, let her mind go ahead, not stop here with herself, but go into the dream of what will happen next. It is the first time she has done this, let her mind go on ahead to the next thing, the journey, the party, the evening ahead. She has been so used to existing in tiny pieces of time, not daring to let herself out of one into another. Always she has been just existing in time's present . . .

Yet not this evening. This evening is different.

What brought about this change, I don't know. Fate. Time weighed up at her back and pushing her on. Her seventeen years now too many to stay a child in, or her father waiting in a room too much darkness for her now when the light, right this minute, is so lovely, so full and warm and golden . . .

Whatever the reason, tonight my mother's thoughts leap into the evening ahead and play there. Even if the man she will meet for the first time tonight had no plans of going to the dance, even if right now he is lying on his narrow bed in his rented room, even if he is sleeping, her need to love him will pull him to his feet, take him to the wardrobe, dress him. Though they've not yet met, her will to fall in love tonight is enough to bring him to the dance.

So, as she slips the dress from its hanger, the thin silk of it slipping over her arms like cream, as she lets the dress fall out around her, stepping into its centre like stepping into a pool, as she draws the dress up around her naked body and feels it touch and settle on the different planes – belly, breasts, the long flat of her back – even as she prepares herself in all these ways my mother knows that tonight will be when time takes her, away from her father's time, into her own time. Like in a myth, the waters will shrivel from her and she will step up, dry, onto the bank, to begin again.

Tonight is when my own father comes to life.

In his narrow bed, lying there with his eyes closed, he also dreams behind his black lashes, his black eyes covered by sleep but dreaming of a young woman who will come to him, who is ready for him, only him. Doesn't all emotion happen that way – thoughts going out first, to touch, then bodies? I even believe my father felt, in the dark heart of his dreams, in the pit of his belly that night, as he opened his eyes, got up from his narrow bed, all the time I believe even he was thinking, "Yes . . . Yes", that time was beginning for him too.

And I see him rise from the bed, pull a white shirt down over his body.

Tonight, he is thinking.

And he smoothes down the front of his shirt with a flattened palm.

There will be a girl . . .

Now my mother, dressed and scented, with even the air around her, and the perfect space under her arms, behind her knees, in the delicate bend of the inside of her elbow, powdered . . . Now she walks back to the mirror a final time. Shoulders, waist, long arms . . . She sees herself in parts, then as a whole. She sees herself as her lover will see her tonight.

Downstairs, in one of the rooms, her father paces and turns. Ankles, her flat soft belly, hands . . .

There is nothing he can do.

Tonight, all these will be places for another man to touch, his daughter's first lover.

Fingertips, cheeks . . .

Tonight, for my mother, finally it will be the end of that other thing. She knows it. Her father knows it. All the nights in the cottage preparing for it . . . That was nothing compared to this. Now she is to go out tonight, and meet a man so dark, with such large hands that he will put on her. It will mean the end of the other thing. And yet . . .

When her father first sees her this evening, stepping into the room where he has been waiting, in her silken dress, with her lips smooth as fruit so he can see them, even from the cold fireplace when she stands at the door, I think how strange it is, and sad and perfect, that my poor mother, when stepping into the room and catching sight of his dark starving eyes, really does think the other thing is over, all that oldness . . .

When, really, the old story is only beginning again, the broken wheel turning slowly on its axle, so for seconds, minutes, it's like a perfect circle and everything has changed, then turns again, another fragment of a degree turns past, turns and begins its broken circle again.

THREE

At the dance where they met, my parents sat together on a tiny sofa. There was the scent from cut roses in a bowl beside them. My father kissed my mother for the first time, deeply like he was drinking from her. Everything, the pink light, the scent of roses, their mouths . . . Everything was soft for her.

Yet even then, when it was early, the roses in their silver bowls were bruised and dying. The stamens had lost their tips of dust, the stems in the water were dry. Out in the dark night insects massed and flew and collected, and my mother didn't sense them out there in the warm air. She didn't feel the touch of a transparent wing, or the movement of a tiny creature's feeler on her young skin.

My father brought her home with him that first night.

He kept her with him in his own rented room, close on the hard bed, still she felt nothing but softness, in their mouths and bodies together, though he was not gentle with her, and his foreign words for her stuck like hooks . . . Still, she felt only softness, she was young. She was a crazy girl for his kisses, that's what my father told her in his bad English. She was crazy for him, for the way he looked at her, for the sounds he made when they lay close together. So different, my mother thought, to those other sounds, his eyes so different from those other hungry guilty eyes.

It seemed simple to her, easy to be in love when everything that happened to her that first night was what she wanted. He wasn't gentle with her, but that was what she wanted. He opened his eyes when he was finished and looked deep into her eyes, and that was what she wanted most of all.

She was seventeen, she had no other time to her. My father was older, and he was used to bodies like hers, hungry little rich bodies that he could turn over and over.

He was expert with her, in touching her delicately so she barely felt it at first. Of course she was going to believe it was love. In the garden, she leaned back against the wall to take the first weight of him, and it was simple. Though there was the insistent movement of insects, a smell of sweetness that is too sweet, a forced flower past its bloom, my mother knew nothing, only his close breath. He leaned into her.

"Darling . . ."

I can imagine what it was like for her, with him so close.

"Darling . . ."

I can feel the press of his heavy body, up against mine.

Of course, it had to be what she wanted.

At home, her father paced the length of the drawing room, up and down, up and down. She knew all the time, he was waiting up for her, returning to the decanter time after time, measuring out the hours that way, waiting, until the cut crystal showed no colour through it. He would never stop waiting for her. No matter how late, no matter how many dark rooms the house contained, he would be awake, be up somewhere in the house, waiting for her. Her knowing, even as she slipped into the house, stepping soundlessly out of her silk dress, slip, stockings, unclipping her bra strap, that he would be coming for her.

"Darling . . ."

There was my own father again, his warm breath in her hair, and his moving hands.

"I love you . . ."

And there was the feel of him in her hands, as my mother's hands moved under him, behind him, to hold him at the nape of his neck, in the soft place where there was no hair. Of course my father had to be what she wanted.

Night after night, after that first night, my father took my mother back with him to the place where he lived, it may have been a room above a shop, or above a bar. And for all the nights her father was waiting. By now he had waited nights and nights, after the parties, and though my mother always came home in the end, she came later and later, until the dawn was in the windows and her father could see himself in the pale light, still waiting in the drawing-room, and he could not come to her then.

That was when it finally ended for him. When he saw the tips of his shoes outlined on the pattern of the drawing-room carpet, and still my mother was not home. It was the night she had run out into the streets – forever. Her father wouldn't wait for her again. He stood for hours looking down at the tips of his shoes, as daylight came into the room and remained there and receded. He stood quietly, very still. He would never see his daughter again . . .

Forever.

Her . . . Would never see . . .

He would never come to the small room where she lived in the end, to take her home.

⁓

I wonder now, in those early weeks, as my father was murmuring in his broken voice to the rich girl, did he know? That there would be no family meeting? No handshake, father-in-law to new groom? No clink of money on the tray after he had made his introduction?

As they packed their bags, bought tickets for the ferry, as his long foreign fingers unbuttoned her blouse, her skirt, did my father guess what it meant to have run out with my mother into the streets? Could he have known then, when he took her with him, that besides her poor undressed body there was nothing else, no other payment due?

My parents married in France, in a funny little seaside town with cheap shops and badly painted cafés where the croissants were kept in large glass jars so they curled and turned brittle in the sunshine and couldn't be eaten. They didn't notice. They were the two people sitting outside at the little table, under the bright yellow sun, not caring that there was nothing to eat. They were the people laughing, my father the man who crumbled a fragment of pastry and threw it at his bride like confetti, sprinkling the brown and yellow flakes thickly in her lap.

"Look at me . . ."

And my mother was the woman who spread her legs wide under her printed cotton skirt, so she could keep the crumbs there for him to eat up, straight up off her sweet deep printed lap, let his tongue take up the crumbs from her, keep them all in his mouth for swallowing.

They stayed in the little town for a while. There was a pebble beach, a pier. Then my father bought a car and they drove around visiting churches and old houses that were locked up but they broke inside and camped there. All my mother's cotton printed dresses became dirty, she didn't care.

"Baby . . ."

She stroked my clean hair as she told me these stories, she was bathing me and so many years had gone by.

"I was so glamorous, then. I was a girl with a handsome man and he was your daddy. I was pretty, my body was very pretty . . ."

I was clean from my bath and in my mind's eye I imagined them, saw them clear as drawings on paper, like I saw people in books at school – always smiling. And there they were, a boy drawing, a girl, they were in a tiny car driving around a country of yellow fields, green, driving all the way through Europe but never to my father's home because he kept saying they were going there, but they never arrived.

They spent months this way, stopping off at village bars in the mountains, or at cafés, staying together in small rooms, sharing a single bed if they could save money, using just one sheet under them.

They swam in cool green river pools during the day, or plunged into the sea, so salty it felt as though it could take the skin off them, or they lay under shady trees or found caves . . . But always coming together in the night in the single bed. Her finding him in the small room that was so black and hot and airless, waiting for the moment when he would turn towards her in the blind room, reach for the outline of her, feel the shape fill in . . .

In cities, they sometimes stayed in grand hotels, my father tanned dark by the sun, my mother sitting up at the bar in faded jeans, her hair tied back with string, ordering cocktails. She wore red lipstick and smiled for everyone, her eyes too bright, her mouth open too wide. My father was right beside her but not close enough. Always she had to move nearer to him, sidling up beside him, moving her bar-stool over, closer, closer, and he started to move away, bit by bit, as she came closer, he turned away from her gaze sometimes, talked to other people. It wasn't like the parties before. Already her smile for him was too wide.

Still, they were having such high times, taking huge bubble baths together in the Ritz, in the Meurice, sleeping for hours in big rooms, with the silk curtains pulled down, breakfast laid out uneaten. My mother still had some money left, and they could spend it.

Forever! She thought.

But the badness had started for my father, it began turning in, and he was beginning to leave my mother sleeping to go out on his own in the afternoons, going to bars to find women, drawing them off to one side, whispering into their ears.

In her sleep, my mother turned, put out her hand.

I don't think she knew he had started that early, she didn't miss him because he was still with her in the night. He still had smiles for her, his lips, dark and wet, still kissed. And her own desire was too strong by now to make her think he didn't come back at her with his own. She was always reaching for him, always feeling for him in the pit of her belly, deep in the part that was hurt from him. Surely that was proof of love enough?

Not long after they came home, my mother received notice that her father had killed himself. There was no will. I was born less than a year later, a silent, uncrying baby.

*

"All the time," she said to me, when she was playing with me, when I was three years old, five, seven, "All the time, you knew what it was like to be a daughter. You were a good baby, you knew how to be so quiet for me. Remember . . ." She was murmuring the words, talking so quietly, ". . . No matter what happens here . . ." She put her arms around my body, ". . . You stay that silent way. No matter what they do to you, that's what a daughter is for . . ." She stroked my hair, a wet rope down my back. She was kissing me, she'd just fixed herself and she was dreaming, she was high.

"We can do anything we want in the end, there's no good or bad, it's only dust. Remember dust will always fill the cracks and openings, it settles on floors. It covers the windows so no one need know anything at all. Remember, darling . . ." Her mouth was moving at my back, her soft, murmuring mouth, ". . . Always to stay that silent way . . ."

———

Before I was born, my father left forever.

He stepped out one night for a pack of cigarettes, as he'd stepped out nights before, staying away until morning, only this time he never came back. My mother started taking more of the pills and injections she had been using with him from the start, first as part of her memory for him, then for sickness, as routine, using them every morning and night, so that it became easier for her to keep them on the tray by the sofa, with her drinks and jug of water, so then she could get to them no matter what the time.

At first she went to the hospital for more prescriptions, then she started going to the streets – she couldn't believe he'd left, couldn't. She kept the skin on the sofa that he'd given her, and lay on it, stroked it, like the dead animal might bring him back. Sometimes she drew the skin right over her like a blanket and lay under it, thinking in her sleep about him, the lovely things he had made her do.

Her first real dealer was the doctor she used most of all, even though she went to other people too sometimes, she kept him near because he always came right to her when I called.

He was an old man, I thought, because he had grey hair, and he was very polite to my mother. He used a soft voice with her, with me. Sometimes when I called him up from the telephone on the landing I found it hard to hear his soft voice on the end of the line.

"Doctor, mummy says, can you come . . ."

At the beginning I stood on a box to reach the telephone. Then later, when I was older, I reached for the heavy receiver and held it. The dirty roses bloomed on the paper around me, at my head.

"She is not feeling well. Can you please bring her a prescription?"

In our room, my mother was shivering under the skin. Her body was like it had arrows going through it.

"Darling, make him come today, make him come now . . ."

From the landing I could hear her talking to me from our room.

I suppose I thought everybody's mother lay down all day, and liked to keep the curtains drawn. I suppose I thought all the children missed days from school when their mothers couldn't open their eyes, or play the game where I had to make her speak.

"Say 'Prescription'" I said to her, because that was the game: to make her speak words before I called the doctor as a test.

"Say it, then I'll phone him, like you said. Say 'prescription' quickly, three times in a row . . ."

"Pre – p – p . . ."

My mother's lips tried to come together to make the shape of the word but they couldn't close or finish, she just puffed out air.

"Pip – p – p . . ."

Her eyes went back in her head she was so tired, they went white. I thought she looked funny then.

I laughed and ran from the room.

"Mummy can't play the game! She can't play the game . . ."

I ran around in circles out on the landing, round and around and around.

"She can't play! She can't play.' But though in my head I heard myself screaming out the words, in the air I wasn't making any noise at all.

I went into the room again. She was lying on the sofa, her head stretched all the way back off the end of it so I could see the long underside of her long neck, white like a gull. How white she was, when she was sleeping. Her neck so long and soft. I went up quietly to her and took away the cigarette that was still burning between her fingers. I think I knew all the time it wasn't a game.

I put my hand on her white neck, I touched it. I felt her little pulse, I had my hand on it, I kept my hand down on it for a while. Then I went back out into the hall and called the doctor who always came. He always came up the stairs and straight into our room.

That night he came with the bag of injections to wake her, only all I could see was that he was putting her to sleep again, always back to sleep again, and she was already asleep. As he drove off in his grey car, the sound of her sleeping filled the room. Her breath going in and out, in and out, louder and louder in our dark room.

From the window I watched the doctor's car drive off down the road making no sound I could hear through the thick glass, only my mother's breath, her huge sleeping breath. My chin rested on the window-sill and I stayed for a long time, looking out. From outside no one could see me there.

He was the first doctor but there were the others who came and fed my mother pills and injected her when she couldn't. She accepted whatever any of the men gave her, it was not always clean, but it had been so long for her that she was used to anything, her body took it all. She had been sick for such a long time that I know now the killing of her started long before the night she died. Long before, with missing one man, that was why her blood thinned and stopped. It was him. He was in her, like a gentle, creeping disease, in her in the story she told, the same story, over and over, of how she loved him.

"We were like angels together . . ." she used to say, and she could never be well. Though she talked about him and for a while it was like she wasn't sad and far-away with pills and dope and crying, as if the knowledge of everything she had done, was made strong with him in her . . . It never lasted. After a while, the disease cooled again, and she fell back into herself again, like she didn't believe any of it was true. Like she'd never had a man to love, only me.

"Poor mummy . . ."

I stroked her hair as the lines of tears ran down her face.

"Poor mummy . . ."

I smoothed back her hair.

"Poor baby . . ."

And in between the stories the men came.

Short men in suits and the tall ones in jeans who looked like cowboys or thieves. Some of them were very young and she let them creep up onto the bed beside her straight away. Others, the ones I didn't like as much, were old with thin, thin bodies and they were frightening, looking at me through their little glasses that their eyeballs filled, staring huge at me so I could see all the tiny red veins, the yellowed whites like egg.

They were such old men I thought they might not stay alive, from the sounds I heard, in the bathroom where I waited for them to finish with my mother, it sounded like she was killing them. Their breath came out ragged and in gasps and they panted too, those old men, like dogs with my mother in the bed, and all the time, I stayed in the bathroom to play. I kept my dolls close. I had them with me in the empty bath, I talked and talked to them so I wouldn't hear, or I took my toys out of the bath and turned the taps on full, so the noise of water would fill the room. I let steam from the boiling-hot tap make the mirror cloudy and the air, so I could pretend I had disappeared.

The men came and went and nothing really changed. I grew a little older, taller. The night my mother died I was eleven years old and full of secrets. I felt then no one would ever know about her, just as she wanted, that I was the only one who could ever know and I would never tell. There was love and sleep and us together in the room, all of her knowledge in me.

As she became weaker, I grew strong.

Every night she brought herself a little closer to the edge.

My father would never come back.

Years and years had passed since the night she drew the silk dress up, stepped into it, in the mirror watched herself . . . Yet the same night the love affair started was the night it started ending. It is how I was made, how I formed in her . . . As my father drew away from her I began to grow. As he unleashed his fingers from hers, unjoined the seam of him to her, turned over . . . As she felt the damp line where their skin had been joined now open to the dry dark air, space widening between them . . . With their separation, I came whole. By the time her lover was gone I was asleep and I was already formed in her, uncurling my finger, feeding through an open mouth so that my own belly would swell. I breathed and lived and fed in all the warm fluids of her blood and tears, birthed amongst them, was milked and protected in them.

The night my mother died, it was only the last pill, only the last gram, but it was enough for her already too full heart.

There was nobody else in the room with her that night, only me, and I was doing the things with her we did most nights . . . I ran her a bath, and I helped her undress, smoothing out the clothes and laying them on the chair so she could find them easily afterwards.

All day she had been well. When I came home from school she had been standing up ironing, she had made a cup of tea for me. There were biscuits in a packet. Her cigarettes were burning in different ashtrays around the room where she'd put them down and forgotten about them, the mug of coffee she had made for herself had a white skim . . . Still. It could often be like that when she was up, and I loved it when she was up.

That day she'd cleaned the room, and shaken out the skin, laid it fresh on the sofa with the other rugs. She had arranged her pills and water neatly on the tray, washed the dishes and, sitting on a plate in the cupboard, there was a cheese sandwich for me to eat later. As she ironed, I read to her from a book I'd brought back from school. My happiness crouched in my heart. The scent of newly laundered cotton filled our room, more than cigarette smoke, more than whiskey, it was the scent of clean clothes, my mother's clothes and mine, that she was making nice for us.

Outside, it was a deep violet winter afternoon, the orange street

lights turned on with a tiny click. It began to rain but we were
warm and comfortable in our room.

Oh, mother . . .

That same afternoon she ironed, stacked the fresh clothes in a neat
pile by the sofa, and I went to the bathroom then, to set the plug in
and turn on both taps. I poured in the milky stuff my mother loved
to bathe in . . . It was what I did most nights. I swirled my hands in
the warm water so the milkiness clouded and foamed. I helped my
mother undress, in all her thinness and lightness, I helped her step
in. The white water came up around her.

While she bathed, I ate my supper, finished the sandwich and
the biscuits. Then I cleared away the iron and the board, put our
nice clothes in the drawer, set my mother's tray close to the sofa so
she could easily get to it. She came out of the bathroom clean and
smelling sweet, and she was pink from the heat of the bath, and
still my happiness crouched in me, it crouched, ready to jump, but
not then, not then because everything was so perfect.

"The water is still hot and lovely," she said to me.

"I've poured more milk into it and there's lots left for you . . ."

She came over to me and reached down for me.

"I love you . . ."

Then one by one she removed my clothes, she took off my
things, slowly, piece by piece, my shirt and my school skirt. She
unrolled the grey socks that I used to wear pulled up high to my

knees, and I sat on the edge of the sofa while she did it, then her hands went under my vest and gently she removed it, in the most careful way she took off my white pants. Then, though I was eleven and too big then for her to hold me in this way, she picked me up and carried me into the bathroom.

I was so close to her.

Her bathrobe was open at the front, and I could feel her beating heart against my cheek. So close. I remember how much of her there seemed, of belly and arms and the chest that contained the beating heart. There was the long length of her body, the expanse of her skin, and she kept me in her arms to carry me right into the warm steamy bathroom with its thick white air, and my mother carried me into that place and placed me down into the warm water and she bathed me. She took a soft cloth and soap and she drew the cloth through every part of me, she squeezed milky water over me and her fingertips moved in my hair, washing me all over, lathering my hair and my legs and all of my body.

It seemed to last forever, her touching me this way, stroking me in a way that was so gentle, it seemed to go on and on and on, the bath swirling milky, and her smoothly moving hands coming under me through the warm water. There was so much love for me, in the white water, it was almost painful for me, almost enough for me to cry out "Mummy!" but I didn't cry out and her hands continued to move in the water, washing me, soaping me, cleaning me. It could not last; that time was all I could have. When she was done, she lifted me clear of the water, wrapped me in a towel, closely like I was a parcel for her, and she took me back, carrying me, to our room.

In our room the fire was on and it was warm and I sat on the floor next to my mother's sofa while she prepared her things for the night. And as I watched the familiar routine, her first two pills, the sip of water in-between, the stuff rubbed on her arm, the new needle taken from its paper packet, the powder melted on the little dish, the needle going in . . . I didn't shiver. Though I was wearing no clothes and already the towel wrapped around me was becoming damp, I didn't shiver. I still felt so warm and full from the bath my mother had given me, only to me. And though I felt a sudden movement at my back as I sat there, beginning to sleep, though I turned and saw my mother jerk upon the sofa, her hands opening and closing, gripping nothing, I still thought we were in our same happy dream and she was warm too and sleepy. And when her whole body jerked again, and her eyes rolled back, maybe I thought she was playing a game because I was frightened then, of her strange face, and her eyes gone back, and her mouth too wide open and trying to close, trying to bite onto something but her tongue caught in the way, and her eyes snapping wide open again and closing and opening, and bits of wet sticking on her chin and lips, and the sound her wide mouth made, coming from in her throat, maybe trying to speak.

I jumped up then and tried to put my hand on her forehead, to stroke it, like I always stroked her forehead, all the other times, but the strength of her jerked my hand away, like she didn't want it, and I was calling "Mummy! Mummy!" like a little girl, calling her over and over like I was helping her but I wasn't helping. I was crying because her breathing was frightening, it was coming in huge rasping holes of breath, and there was wet coming out of her mouth too, and one of her eyes was closed and the other was wide open and round . . . I ran out into the hall.

"Mummy! Mummy!"

I was crying out, shrieking the words.

"Mummy!" and maybe some people heard, maybe they came running, up the stairs, the people who lived above us, maybe they heard, I don't remember. I remember standing at the telephone and though I was still shouting "Mummy!" still I could dial the number the doctors had given me, and I called the hospital as people came from upstairs and from downstairs in the house, as they went running into our room, I had already told the man on the phone where to send the ambulance.

It seemed like a long time I was out on the landing, out of our frightening room, and there were people all around me, and they seemed to be around me for a long time, but when at last I went back into our room everything was quiet.

Perhaps there were people there, I can't remember.

It was very quiet.

I didn't look at the sofa, I went to the window and I stayed there, I waited there until the sirens came. I didn't want to look at her then, on the sofa, in case she started moving again. It was dark. We hadn't turned any of the lights on inside, only the light from the bathroom still showed across the hall, a thin strip of yellow. Outside it was winter, the sky was hard black, and then the ambulance came and suddenly there was colour, there was the flashing of the police light, that blue light, and there was the ambulance and the siren screaming I could hear even through the thick glass of the window, and the light making our room go into deep red.

On–off, the dark light showed red and black.

On–off.

As my hands went up to the glass they were red too, red hands, and then I turned and saw my mother lying there and she was red in the flashing lights, and then black, and then she was red and then she was cold blue, and all the time the siren was screaming, it was crying, and though I knew what had happened and my mother was so still, though the lights flashed in her open eye, and the scream of the siren was so loud and she was so still, just then I couldn't feel sad, or tears. All I could feel was my skin, taste the sweetness of my skin left from the milky stuff she'd let me have in the water, the soft touch of my skin where my mother had bathed me. That's what came to me then, what she had done to me came back to me then, and that is what I thought about, not the thing lying on the sofa, not that.

Perhaps that is why, when the ambulance men came, I didn't mind. Because I felt my mother all through my body then, I didn't mind, the daughter didn't mind. Her mother had gone but she had stayed with her, was warm with her, had the taste of milk and sweetness. She was inside.

She heard her mother in the sirens and it was herself she heard.

Second Part

Dust Comes

He lights a match. For a second, she sees his face illuminated by the flame, for a second there's the face. Then it's gone. It's black again, and the woman is cold again, like before.

She is kneeling somewhere on the hard floor. There is a man in the room with her, the man with the tiny flame in some corner, by the door, or at her back. She can hear his breathing in the dark, she can smell the scorch of his little matches that he loves to use in the dark.

"I'm here . . ."
He lights another.

"And here . . ."
Now he's somewhere else.

"And here . . ."

And somewhere else, moving around the room unseen while she remains in place on the floor, weighted there, and her hands are kept together as he has wrapped them, with oiled chains. If it was light, she would see how they have marked her.

Sometimes in this position she seems to wait for hours. It is not hours but all time is swallowed by the blackness in the room. It is so late at night no one in the world could be awake. She can hear the man taking off his clothes, his breathing heavy, ragged because he is so old he will be dead soon. She hopes he will be dead soon, though she needs him, waits for him. She hopes he will leave her alone this time but he won't leave her alone. He can't stop himself, his huge hand at her breast, his dark mouth coming closer, opening, until she can smell the old breath coming out of him, like out of a black bag.

Still, she continues to kneel for him. She wants to be so pretty kneeling for him, her skin exposed for him, the outline of her bones. So pretty with her hair down her back a rag, though she's been starved by him and now her teeth are too big in her face, and her eyes are flat and dead. Still, she continues to kneel, and he stands somewhere in the room, smoking, lighting match after match and letting them drop with sparks of flame, on the floor, in her lap, in her hair. If she could see his face again, lit up for a second like before, that might be a sign: *Start with me . . .*

Instead it's dark, and in the dark spaces between the matches she could be alone in the room it's so quiet. Perhaps she's asleep and it's only her breath she hears, no one else with her. Only her shallow air, and that's all there is in the big house, in all the locked rooms in the big dark house, her draw of air the only movement. If a person walked down the narrow street outside they would see no light at any of the windows, hear no sound. They would think that the house was empty, nobody in it to keep knives. A person walking outside would not think about love taking place behind the walls, behind the glass. They would not consider a deserted house could harbour the damage of that emotion.

After all, the woman is unknown.

There is no family, she has no friends. She came back to the city in autumn and though the streets were familiar, there was a café she used to visit . . . She could live in any house now and no one would guess it. Only the man who keeps her knows where she is. There's only him to look after her, feed her soft cheese at night, make sure her sheets are clean. He has her safely and she won't leave now; he has the belt with him as proof. It has taken all the other feelings out of her, created her empty and hungry, and he's the only one awake in the middle of the night, in this empty house, to fill her.

Start with me . . .

This is what she has now, hunger beyond the hold of normal appetites. She opens her mouth in the dark as if to speak, but she won't speak.

Start with me . . .

She opens her mouth for thirst, for taste . . . But these are nothing compared to the particular appetite he's created in her.

Start with me now . . .

She forms the words, says them in her own mind, because she would never ask him. And she pulls the chain up hard between her wrists to cut them, because that small pain is better than waiting for him. It's the waiting that keeps her breath coming quickly in the dark; once he's started it's just like feeding, it's simple then. Like the kind of need that's grown in the darkest places, where crippled animals are kept, or plants that are forced back into the earth . . . One glimpse of a tiny light and for all these things the fraction of life left in them will leap towards it, trying to grow.

That is the method used with her by this man: Keep her in, where no one can see. Keep her in a room all day, keep her sleeping, leave her on her own all day in a bed, lying there, not moving much so her bones get softer, like milk. Leave her in a big house all day where no one visits and watch how she comes to love you, just like the others. Waiting for you to come home at night, her skinny arms wrapping around your neck like string, and like with string you have to cut her down.

Start with me . . .

That's the method for the man, the woman.

Start with me . . .

Mother, daughter. Father, lover. It's the same no matter who they are. Perhaps this man is the same man my mother married, or he is another man, but either way he is the same.

"You will notice, doctor . . ."
    The man has a young woman up on the examination table.
    "She is not in pain . . ."

The doctor draws back the bloodless rim of an eye, shows the pale iris, the whites like the woman is sleeping. Then, with his other hand, gently he inserts an instrument into the space that the man has made inside her.

"You will see . . ."

He probes further insider her, but there's nothing there. As if acid has eaten out the interior, left her with nothing, a gap.

"There can be nothing wrong at this stage, surely," the man says. He has paid to say it. "A little damage, of course, you will notice in certain areas, but she has no pain. And young women of this age are apt to damage. They are quite clumsy with themselves, they don't take care . . ."

He coughs.

The doctor withdraws the instrument.

"Is she eating regularly," he says. "In these cases, hysteria, self-dramatisation . . . That's often the case. You're the father?"

The older man, standing to one side in the surgery, nods.

"I am her father."

"Well, then," the doctor turns away. "You'll do whatever you want, I suppose . . ."

He goes to the basin in the corner and begins to wash his hands. As if he can clean himself from the things the man has shown him in his daughter, this young woman with her white skin, with her long red hair. As if.

*

133

Now, in the dark, the man takes the matches again. There's the tiny scrape of the tip of a match against tinder, it catches, and it flares for a second to lighten the room, then goes out.

As if.

From the other side of the room the woman waits for him. He can feel her waiting, in the frailty of her breath, trying not to breathe, on the floor at her knees like the flat blade of a knife. He knows her exact shape in the dark, the swell of her lip, the little bones running down the length of her spine like ornaments.

Everything about her he knows.

The doctor stands with his back to the older man and lathers the white soap in his hands, lathers it thick and creamy but still he feels he can't get the stain off from what he has seen. The girl is young, and the man has kept her in so no one can see what he's done to her over time. Not even the man's sons know what he's done. The doctor lathers and lathers his hands. As if trying to wash away something that cannot be made clean is the most normal thing in the world.

"Of course," he continues, with his back to the man and young woman in the room, "I'm only guessing. Other things could be wrong, psychological. You say your wife died when the girl was very young . . . That could be why you think she seems unhappy now. The loss of interest, the fact that she has no friends . . . Grief ignored has different ways of showing later, and now she's growing

134

up . . . *If you like, I can refer you to someone. You could take her —"*

"No, no," *The father interrupts, impatient. "She doesn't need anyone like that."*

He turns to the frightened young woman, half-dressed. Her hair is all down over her face.

'Put your clothes on," *he says. "There's nothing we can learn from this man."*

So, with some blood still coming out onto the white examination sheet, the woman lifts herself up, gets dressed. She gets dressed around the hurt, moving herself carefully around it so it doesn't touch. She is weak, she has not been eating. She wanted to eat, for a time, but her father didn't want it for her. He wanted to see the row of bones in her, not blood coming out, wounds, any of this. He wants light bones, not a woman, a girl. He pushes the hair back from her face. He doesn't want any hair on her.

Now, quietly, the man comes to her where she kneels on the floor. He touches the top of her head, lightly, so lightly she could hardly feel it. His hand on her head feels weightless, like a shell. He keeps it there, on her, and knows his hand is trembling. Sometimes he is frightened by how careful he wants to be with her, how carefully he wants to keep himself apart from her as if he could stop himself, as if he could control this thing.

How old are you?

*

135

He had asked her the first time they met. The rose light from the café glass was over her face and she looked like a tiny child.

How old?

He had planned it so they could meet there, in the light of coloured glass. He would seem more attractive to her there.

He had looked at her then, wanted to touch her then, lightly, the way he is touching her now on her young head. She was so . . . beautiful. In the way the other was, the same afraid movements, quickness. The same pale eyes that always tried to see more than there was to see. This one had illness about her, something in her not used to people . . . He could fix that. The other one had been like that too, in the beginning.

How old are you? he had asked, that day, the first time.

But he didn't need to ask. He knew, she was the right age, she was what he wanted.

That was how he started again, with her, so long ago it seems, but really not so long. And now she is near perfect, light as breath. She is the way he wanted her to be, and she is quiet and good. She is like the other one in that way, so silky. Even after he has given her all the pills so he can leave her lying there, she could still move her tongue a little and give him pleasure if he wanted it. Like a little piece of wet silk for him to wipe himself with.

✳

"What is this?" A man she has never seen before probes the swelling with gentle, expert fingers. "What do I find here?"

"Nothing . . ."

It is years earlier and the young woman is still a child. Eight years old. Nine years old. She is lying in her own bed, in her room at home and a strange man is touching her.

"Nothing . . ."

She looks away from him, looks further away from the father's eyes.

"Nothing. Please don't look any more. I feel well."

"She's lying, doctor," the father says. His voice makes her look at him, and when she does, he keeps her in his eyes. The shape of her laid out on the sheet . . . She has seen it so often reflected in her father's dark eyes.

"She's lying," he says to the doctor again. "There's something wrong with her, I'm sure. She's hurt herself . . ."

The doctor comes in closer, to see. He probes again the swelling, so tenderly, gently. To the little girl he whispers, so the father will not hear, "Did you do this yourself?"

But the girl begins to cry.

"Nothing, nothing," she is crying. She is very young.

"Please don't look at me . . ."

In the dark room, standing above her, the man lights another match. Then, as quickly, he puts it out on his tongue. He does not want to frighten her. She is not strong, and he needs her with some strength. He has not been giving her enough food and in the meantime the other appetite has been growing, enlargening in her; it is eating her out. He has to keep her calm, unmoving in the darkness. If she walks across the room, the sight of her putting one foot carefully in front of the other is enough to make him turn away. And if he sees her, as, by mistake, one morning when he saw her, he knows he will be sick right there in the room. To see, in the light, the thing he's made of her.

"I would say, at a glance, your daughter simply needs feeding up."

The doctor says the words. This man brings his daughter to him, to pay him, to hear these kinds of words.

"There's clearly some form of obsession, with her food," he says. "Have her spend some time with other women, if possible. Do you have a sister?"

The father shakes his head.

"Any women friends she could stay with for a time?"

Again the father shakes his head, no.

"Well then, you must be responsible for her . . ."

The doctor is, all this time, as he speaks, still trying to clean his hands. From the first examination, and the second, and the third . . . He retains them, these unclean hands. Lying hands that pretend to feel no damage.

"Well, then . . ."

He does not look at the young woman on his table, with her bleeding, and her awful bones.

"You must take her home and keep her safe with you . . ."

That seems a long time ago to him now, when he last saw her during the day. It is winter now, it has been winter for a very long time.

She kneels at his feet in the darkness like a little cat.

And he lights a match. He puts it out.

For years he has been searching for her.

It was not all he was doing, but even when he was with other women he was always looking for her, waiting for that moment when their eyes would meet, as, he believes, she had been looking for him, too. Of course, once he found her he would prepare meticulously to keep her. Once he had her in the house, and the door shut . . . Then, he thought, his plan would be to never let her go. His breath wouldn't disgust her then, when his breath was all she knew, nor his dark filthy rooms. The plan would be to keep a white room for her in the top of the house, sun comes in there. She will like it there.

You must take her home and keep her safe with you . . .

The plan would be to keep her there, where she feels safe. For a while he will continue with his courtly ways, combing the black

139

through his hair, taking her on his knee. He will tell her stories, undress her very carefully for bed at night, he will make love to her in ways that are always new to young women, and she will be excited by him, by his close attention. She will never leave him.

Darling . . .

She will never want to go.

Now he strokes the fine hair on her head, remembering. Strokes the hair clean back from the face, the long neck clean of strands. He knows how carefully, over time, he has prepared the body for himself, no one else . . . More and more keeping food from it, making it lie still.

Through the autumn he used to dress it, cover it with a slip, a dress, there were layers of clothes. Sometimes then he used to take the body out at nights, when it was dressed, her lovely face was painted on. The lights from a million tiny bulbs reflected in her eyes as they stood outside in the dark before entering and when they were inside, the restaurant he brought her to was always expensive, but he had prepared her so she could sit there at the table, in the expensive clothes he had dressed her in and no one would know she had lived for so long in a hospital. He used to bathe her himself in those early months. He had the pallor of her skin just right. He bathed her in milk and soap every night, preparing the skin so it no longer looked lit by fluorescence, hospital walls. He remembers as he strokes her smooth skin now, the sliding feel of her body in the water, the oil of bath milk and soap. Thin strands of pale hair combed by the water's long ripples, courses, folds.

All this is what he wants to do always, to keep her. Use money and food, giving, then taking away . . . Use the trust of warm water. All through the autumn to the beginning of winter he took her out and gorged her on expensive food, made her face soft with all the custards and creams, melting chocolates and white sauces . . . And then later, when the season turned very cold, took the food away, waited for the dents and hollows to form, for her teeth to become large in her face.

For now, in his plan, it is safe to starve her. She is kept indoors now. By now, she is used to his touch, all the motions of his hands, the scent of him, his false black head in her lap and the citrus smell of his hair oil coming off on her fingers when she runs them through his hair. She is used to his plan, when he wants to sleep, when he wants to rouse himself. She is used to the vain pattern of damp bandages he wears wrapped over his torso, criss-crossing through his groin, bound around the top of his thighs . . . Binding him together like a puppet only there is skin underneath the muslin, not wire and cloth. She touches him beneath the wrappings and skin comes off, it scatters in flakes in the bed.

She knows all these secret things about him. She has been with him so long her limbs feel part of his limbs when he holds her, the parts where he is dry the raw parts of her own body. The belt she gave him to wear he keeps strapped tightly around his waist when he is undressed of all other clothing. She knows how he straps it, how it leaves a mark. She knows the way he picks daintily at his food like a woman, the way he takes up a cigarette in the middle of a meal, pushing his plate to one side and, while still chewing, lights it. She is used to the vulgarity of him, sucking a piece of food from his tooth, the way he would reach under the damask tablecloth in expensive restaurants to put his hand up her.

In the dark he sees her, with a dark glass eye. He has put all this knowledge in her so now it is winter there is nothing left of him that could sicken her. She will never want to leave him. The puppet has her. The arm swings. The puppet knows everything.

He knows when to eat and sleep, knows the times when he shouldn't touch the woman's body, when he should leave the body alone. He knows what the body needs before the body knows. The sponge of water to press against the mouth . . . He knows when this is to be done, just as he knew when autumn was over and he no longer dressed the body to take her out, when the winter came and he knew to bring the body inside for the last time, lay her in the quiet room at the top of the house. He knew she would lie there in the white room, on the bed, he always planned it that way. That she would be very still. Then she would hear the turn of the key in the front door and a smile would form on the body's face then, the only movement, thinking puppet master was home again.

He fixed it.

*

He wanted a place where he could live, act out love, desire, a room where no one could see him remove the cloth from his body, undo the shirt, tear open the front of thin trousers to let his insides spill out.

Now it is late in winter and he has made everything simple for the body. To cut the hair when the hair needs cutting. To wash the hands. To feed yellow custard when the body is weak, even though the mouth can't hold most of it, with a spoon he pushes the custard in full.

He wants to keep the body alive. He doesn't want sound from it, but he wants the legs to work, the body to respond. He wants the body under him, to manipulate, or to lay out, or he wants the body up against the wall, or on the table where insects crawl, beside his knife and fork and plate . . . He wants that most of all. To sit in a little chair at the table and be a visitor to this room. To sit quietly and in time, see the body's eyes close, the colour roll away so he can see the whites like little fish beneath the lids. Always he is excited to see the little fish. That is when he can do anything with the body at all.

This is what he is thinking now, now the matches are gone, burnt in her, in the floor, or dead as they went down.

Anything at all . . .

She still crouches at his feet, makes no sound. That's how well he has trained her. He removes his hand from her head and with great gentleness puts his fingers in her eyes to make the little fish. His long fingers do it, like soft hooks, to make it like she is sleeping. He is fastidious in the things he does, in his attentions. Though it is getting worse for her, though he has made her worse, still there are times when he picks up the body all of a piece, like a length of cloth, like white linen he has in his arms to stitch and cut and shape, to save.

He gathers her up like this, she's so light, like linen, and, because the fish eyes will show for the rest of the night now, and he can do anything he wants to with the body, very gently he has her in his arms and lays her down on the bed, and though the body is still, her head moves and when he takes his hand away from her, walks away from her, the head keeps moving as she turns this way, and that way, to try and discover where he is in the room. She can't see, but he can see. Everything about her he knows, and he loves the way he can see, and she can't see.

The doctor in the long white coat comes up close to her again. There have been many doctors in the hospital but he is nicer than the others. He is holding something behind him.

"A surprise . . ." he tells her. "Can you guess?"

He sits down beside her, then he brings out a teddy bear from behind his back.

"Will you look after him for me?"

She nods, "I will look after him," and she takes the little bear and holds him tightly, tightly.

"Now," the doctor says. *"I want you to tell me where it's sore . . ."*

He is an old man and he doesn't ever want her to see. He has become so ugly, when once he was firm and pretty, when all his teeth were white, when his eyelashes were thick against his lover's cheek . . . Now, no young woman should see him. He never goes outdoors without a hat pulled down low, dark glasses. He is never without a scarf wrapped high around his ragged neck. By now he has kept her in the room at the top of the house for so long she is trained not to see him in daylight, not see what she's doing, running her young tongue into the dry insides of his grey mouth, over yellow teeth, licking, kissing. He only wants touch, for her to want him. Only think of him as something she wants all the time.

That's why he comes to her room only at night. He can believe then that by leaving before it is light she won't see the lines on his face, deep and discoloured where the make-up has collected, won't see how dye stains the skin of his head, collects in clumps at the roots of his wispy hair. He can believe she only sees the lovely way the pale shapes of his hands move over her, the hands a barber has attended to so that even though veins push through like roots beneath the skin, and brown spots grow there, still they are soft from the barber's ointments and very beautiful to the touch.

"Touch me and see . . ."

*

145

Come on honey. Come and step outside with me.

He wants her to see his handsome clothes, like he wore the day he met her, expensively woven in cashmere and wool . . . He wants her to see them in the dark light from the window, not his thin body with no muscle or heavy blood left in it. Touch the fabric of expensive suits, not a caving chest, and the few prickly grey hairs that grow there.

You know, I've been watching you for a long time.

From the first day he wanted to see her, and her not see. He knew then his bandaged body would be nicer for her than his skin. He knew how, in the darkness of his house, he could seem exciting to her, and young, how he could be like a knife.

"In parts I am still perfect," he whispers into the air around him, and she can hear the soft voice, the words.

"My pointed fingernails, my finely wrapped body, neat as a girl's, and my hard arms are still good, and white as yours . . ."

She lies quietly on the bed, and her head turns and turns towards the words.

"I have wine in my mouth," he whispers, and she doesn't need eyes to see his words, ". . . Chablis, black burgundy . . ."

Her head moves on the bed, the air of his words moves around her.

"You can taste wine when I kiss you," he whispers. "Not my stomach. Wine, not old breath . . ."

At that second, he is down on her, close on the bed, his smooth hands are upon her.

"You want me to come to you," he whispers, and his darkness is on her face, in her ear. "You want me to make it easy. You want me to smell and touch you, close your eyes, taste the bitter smoke of my cigarette, feel my fingers in your hair . . ."

Then his breathing pulls away. He moves from her, she hears footsteps in the room, there is silence, long stillness . . . Then he returns, the soft words return.

"I light a match and it's easy," say the soft words.

"I smoke, I'm standing in a corner of the room, perhaps, or right next to you, behind your little back bent over like a reed, standing over you while your fish eyes stare blind and your head threshes on the bed . . ."

She turns again. She wants to move towards the words, have them.

"I stand here," they say, "and I smoke and I let you wait. Let me smoke, while you wait. Let me smoke through this cigarette, start another. Light matches, let you wait. Let me leave you there on the bed to wait. I want you to faint with cold while I smoke. I want you to fall onto the hard floor, cut your face open like a pomegranate spilling its seeds. I want to keep you lying there with your poor eyes out, waiting, your cut face. I want you there, laid out, on the bed, on the table. You're so precious to me, your bones are meat I want to suck, I want the sweet marrow."

The cigarette burns, the ash falls thickly, and it burns and burns. Though the room is cold the man burns. Fever. Age. He'll be dead

147

soon. His thoughts consume him, his vanity. He hates this thing with him here kneeling in the room, he loves it. When, finally he comes down on her she rises, she is all mouth, teeth. She is red and maw-mouthed, and he'll try and get her all, there's nothing else in the room but her body and though he tries to get her all, she has him in her body. Her openings, swallowing him, are huge.

All the past and present consume him then, when she is eating him up. All time becomes this time: all women, this one woman. He feels it, all the women inside her. One rises for him through the dark, towards his row of yellow teeth, towards all the pain and burning, rising, like flame, and as she comes up another falls, crumpling from him, fading. She fades and fades. There is the smell of scorch and burn. No more pain.

"There is nothing inside me, doctor . . ."

The little girl wants to whisper it, the woman wants to.

"He's left space inside, and it's dark there . . ."

The doctor dries his hands. Then he goes to his desk and writes out a prescription.

"Help me," the girl wants to say, the woman wants to say.

"He is killing me . . ."

But the doctor simply tears the prescription from the pad and hands it to the father.

It is dawn.

Pale tissue light.

The man has gone from the room and from where I lie on my bed I have become a container, only a vessel for the others, they are in me. Here is my mother as a child lain out in a doctor's white room, another who is the girl standing by the window, her breath on the cold glass. Another woman wakes in a quiet room, in papery light, another sleeps on the sofa, an animal's skin at her back but her body so light it makes no indent upon it.

"I loved him," she is murmuring, and it's my lips that form the words.

"We were so happy, we were so in love . . ."

I feel my mother closing her eyes, falling, closing her eyes, sleeping, then rising up in a rush, as if her lover is there in the room with her, rising towards him, her body wanting to have every part of him inside her so he can't hurt her again.

"Start with me!" the shape of her body cries, opened for him like a hinge, but though her body cries it the room is quiet. The woman falls back again.

I lie still on my bed, as rag, as the cut skin, and women continue their pattern, they turn, and they turn . . . Mother. Daughter. They rise, they fall, the same. Repeating is a truth of nature, like one flat cloud forms in the sky after its sister. They are not identical, but in the blue sky they are the same. I see myself, the daughter, continuing in a blue sky, another, my mother, drifts before me, my dream. Her love smiles are the same as mine, same pale eyes closing when pleasure slowly runs down through her veins. In the country of my mother I am her true native. Stranded in another country, when I want to remember her, I only have to look at me.

I imagine I am my mother, feel my heart in my throat as I hear my father's soft tread coming down the hall. I hold up a dress in the mirror and it trembles. Then his footsteps stop, outside my bedroom door, but it is late afternoon and there is gold light everywhere in my room and nothing can happen to me now. The footsteps continue down the hall, become softer, further away. The dress I hold before me is white silk, I hold it before me, over my body as if I am already in it, the waist and hem and neck of it against my skin like a touch. When I have it on I shine in the last of the gold light. I go out in it to meet the man I will marry.

"We were so happy," I say to the child at the window.

"We were so in love . . ."

I lie fully back across the sofa: I am her. I want to wear my white dress again, feel my smooth face pressed for a kiss. Though I am frightened of the men, I want them all: The father who comes in the night, the lover who is cruel, the husband who is cruel. Only the high pear-tree outside my bedroom window is safe. As I stand in my mother's lovely golden room, in the house with many windows where she grew up, I am her. My heart, hers, crying out to the tree, to the clean gold air to keep me safe.

But in the end, nothing can protect me against who I will become. It is fixed, like the branches of the tree are fixed like wire in winter. In the end I am left alone, in a quiet room left, the gold gone, a dark house for a home. The summer is gone, and the pale wine sparkling in a glass that is like a flower. Long shadows lie on the lawns . . . And so much time has passed, and for so many years my mother has been dead, she's been buried in wet earth, and yet still I remember, white silk, warm light on my skin at summer's end, as if these are my own memories.

Here, in this deserted house, in this room, it is as if I have her full in me, her stories, memories, all the women. I am at the mirror, folding back my hair, or sitting outside in a café with my yellow skirt spread wide to catch the crumbs for a man to eat up off me . . . Or I am lying in my white room, falling softly to sleep, as she used to sleep, with a worn skin at my back and a child sitting upon it, stroking the dry hairs as if for comfort.

There, there . . .

Drifting into sleep . . . All the women.

There, there . . .

Light deepens, warmth fills the room.

There, there . . .

There, there . . .

And warmth comes, tiredness comes.

*

There, there . . .

And in the warmth and tiredness I can begin to dream.

All the women open their mouths and when their breath catches their eyes roll back and they begin to dream.

I see everything then.

I go through his house like an angel, floating above the bare floors. In sleep the doors are not always locked and rusty for me, in sleep I touch the handle, the flakes of rust won't corrode my skin, I turn the handle and it turns to meet me. I push the heavy door with the strength in both my arms, a crack, then a little more and I push again and the creaking door breaks its seal to swing in on the room within.

Inside, the air of the room comes upon my face like sweet and rotted breath, and warm. Old air. Thick flaps of cloth hang silently at the large windows and let no brightness in, but the heat of years of sunshine is banked up behind them, staining the white linen yellow, staling the air like old women's breath. As my eyes grow accustomed to the light I see this is a room of old women, sitting around a table, a beautiful table set with candles and dishes and silver, and these ladies are sitting around the table, but they don't move. Their hands rest by their plates like claws, set with the heavy stones of rings. Thin velvet slippers hang from their tiny feet.

They seem to sit there waiting for something. Their long dresses pile in folds on the floor. Their hair is dusted white and stuck with pearls, jewels . . . They are so old they could be dolls, but softer to the touch, with soft stuff in them. As I come closer I hear tiny puffs of air, like breath, like the breath of spore that grows in the darkness and when shown to the air corrupts into dust. I hear that same sound all around me, the dolls decaying in the draught of air I have brought into the room. It is the sound of their skin and stitching and stuffed insides turning into air and I reach for the door but I can't reach the door. The smell of the dolls is rotting and sweet, like sweet earth, but warm too, in my nostrils and mouth, and it fills my mouth with the sweet earthiness so my mouth is full of it, like cake.

It is the sweetness of their dried organs, the dust of kidneys and hearts and intestines. It is the smell of dried moisture trapped down amongst the wrappings of their clothes, passages opened with mould that settles, in time, to a thick powder. I see one doll head tip forward with the force of new air, and another. Slowly, one by one, all the dead ladies tip their heads towards their empty plates, they are falling, their joints loosening, the internal bindings that have been holding them are falling apart, and the belly drops now, the dry stomach contents are excreted onto the floor. Bits fall from their nostrils, from their ears.

Now I see their hair is not dressed, it is dust, a few glittery ornaments left stuck in the pile. It is not beautiful, or scented, only dust, a nest, like the dry collectings in the corner of an empty room. When I look closely I see the remainders of rouge worked into their doll faces, but their eyes have gone, and their mouths are open and black. They have had to wait too long for their lover. He invited them in, here to wait in this room and he served them plates of bones now picked clean, poured them yellow fluid into their crystal glasses that once was sweet wine. He has left them here too long. For hundreds of years they have had to wait for him to return but it has been too long since the sound of his footsteps in the hall, his key turning in the lock. Too long since his quiet fingers played amongst their hair.

Start with me . . .

I touch a hand that rests on the table.
It is my hand.

Something moves behind my back. I start to turn but a thin white arm comes out around me. I can't move.

"You see?"

His arm draws me closer in, closer. Then slowly he lowers his face down beside me. His painted eyes, painted mouth . . . Smiling with red lips. "You see?"

The thick cloths at the window let in no air. There's his face at my face, and there's the smell of the room, and his arm tight like wire around me, and I hold my breath while reaching for the door, feel it swing outwards . . . Then see only black.

When she wakes, after the bad dream, it's dark again. The man has come back to be with her again, he is somewhere in the room.

All the day has gone. Behind the bare window a grey moon shows, and the orange sodium of street lamps, and she sees him standing there, silhouetted there by the dark glass, delicate as a paper cut-out. Children could look up from the market below, and see the glass window of the high room as a stage, and him as a thin paper man, with threads pulled on a stick to make him move, to make him jerk and twist his head, jump, come down.

This is the thing he is.

She saw it from the beginning, when she looked into his brightly coloured face she knew, into his glass eyes, his hair that was black as if it was painted on . . . In the dream she saw it.

I remember, doctor . . .

In the dream there were all the others, all his lovers. In the dream she knew . . . That he had touched their false hair like he touches her hair. That he had arranged them, their legs, their arms, in patterns that would please him.

He had turned the head of one of them to see herself in the mirror.

"Can't you see," he said, "how beautiful she is?"

It was a dream but this is what he wants. She knows it, that he wants to keep her, like he keeps the others, like a lover, like a new bride, like a daughter he may come for in the night . . . It was a dream but it's what he wants, to keep her like he keeps them. To keep her safe.

I remember . . .

He wants her body opened out, transformed, made into an emblem, something to keep and put with all the others.

"Can't you see," he will say to her then, and he will turn her own face to the mirror, "how beautiful you are"

He has come to her, she knows, like he came to all the others, to use love, desire, all the little knives to use on her to create this thing, a body he can keep inside, sit up, lie down. He wants a finger running down her face like a blade, her wounds healing in such a way a doctor would heal them – a row of dainty stitching on her skin somewhere, an organ removed or altered. To make her like the others . . . To make her the same as them . . .

It's what he wants. She wants it. The cut, the fine, fine threads that no one else can see.

And yet –

I remember, doctor . . .

There is this voice in her, this child – *I remember it all . . .*

She knows exactly the game they are playing together. The poor creature by the window needs to play it, she, lying on the bed with her eyes cleaned out, needs to play.

*

She has spent all her life waiting for this.

And yet —

I remember, he came into my room . . .

She came back to the city because she was looking for him, for the thing her mother wanted . . . To be like her, to be with her . . . That memory was already in her and she wanted to keep it, like a long pin to turn in on herself, to make the memory real.

And yet —

And all the years she waited, under fluorescent lights, in hard hospital beds and now at last she has it back, her mother's life embedded in her —

And yet —

Her mother's life taken root by its hook —

Doctor, I couldn't see, but he hurt me . . .
He said he wouldn't hurt me, but he hurt me . . .

There was that moment when he moved his hand and let the white dress fall, the moment of it slipping in a pool on the floor around them, deep at her ankles like milk and a man's dark fingers in it, using it later as bandage, to wipe her.

He left space inside me.
There's nothing there.

*

So now he comes towards her in the dark room, and she kneels for him on the floor like she always kneels for him but tonight the game will be more real than before.

"There is something I would like . . ." he says.

And she knows now, exactly, what he wants. She wants it.

"There is something . . ."

And he comes to her quietly, there is silence all around him. On the table, a jangle of coins, a crumpled note, a few pieces of uneaten food crumbled on the top . . . He pushes these aside.

And he puts his hand at her back, drawing her up from the floor, pressing harder now, more urgently, he whispers to her and his breath is sour.

"There is something . . . But you must promise me you want it too."

Like that day, the first time when he led her, out onto the street, down through the market to his house, like when he unlocked the front door and pushed her softly inside, so he leads her now, pushes her now. Like that day with all the boxes crowded the dark hallway, he began to kiss her, and the taste of him then was sour, so the taste of him now is sour, though to kiss her is not what he wants to do now.

Without talking, like before when he brought her up the stairs, onto the dark landing, and up beyond it, he pushed her, gently, so now he brings her up onto the table, and like before, when the air seemed to grow colder with every floor she ascended, and darker, and more close at her face, so now she is cold, no warmth in her.

Past closed doors that day he brought her where he wanted, up another flight of stairs to the top bedroom and inside it was dark, and there he removed his coverings – the scarf and wrappings – so, like then, he lays these down on the floor beside him. Like then when there were no lights and she could only see the man as a shadow, but heavier than a shadow, with huge hands, so now she sees him in the darkness.

"Promise me you want this, too . . ."

Like before his breath was whispering, like he's whispering now, and she wants what he wants, she has always wanted it –

And yet –

Help me doctor!

She wants to cry out.

Help me!

And his face is above her where she lies on the table, and like she remembers that day, it seems so long ago, how his puppet body was huge, he was wasted with age that was eating him – but the puppet was huge . . .

"Anything you do for me," he whispered, that day, long ago, with the musty sourness of his breath like he's whispering now.

"Is our secret . . ."

And his face comes over her now, and she tastes his mouth again, his dyed face pushed up against hers, and like that day, the first time, when he gathered her hair back with one hand, and pulled it back so her neck was bent back and her body was bent back like a bow, and she was pliable for him, held in place but flexible as a bow, as an arc, a bridge for him to lay himself upon . . . So he arches her on the table now.

"Anything . . ."

Like before, and she wanted it –

And yet –

And like that day, when he delayed a little longer, playing with her hair, the line of her throat, so he waits now, his long fingers caressing her throat.

"Anything, anything."

His voice like a beating drum.

"You promised me."

And like then on her neck where he had laid it exposed, the little secret pulse is beating, and, like he took up a silk scarf then, so he takes up something now, something like cloth to use on her.

"There, there . . ."

But it is not cloth he uses.

"There there . . ."

She can feel it, the dry touch of it, and he has it gathered up around her, he is not wiping her, he is not making her clean but he is wrapping it around her, this dry thing, folding it like it may be a garment upon her, around her shoulders, on her back –

"Anything . . . Anything . . ."

And yet –

I remember . . . I remember.

There's this voice.

She hears the child crying.

Help me! He is killing me!

And it's like their first night together.
"Can't you see how beautiful you are?"
The dress dropped from her like milk.

And she screams.

No!

It's the skin he uses. It's her mother's thing.

And she screams again.

No!

Again. Again.

No!

She doesn't want it.

*

And the puppet leaps back. The scream fills the air.

He runs from the room.

⌒

Hours pass in darkness, or minutes. Pulse by pulse her blood comes back.

Slowly, she lifts herself up on the table. She can't see where the man is in the room. One of her eyes is closed like a seam and liquid comes from it, it trickles down her cheek like crying, hardens into salt, dried blood. On her arms and legs and belly a field of purple blooming shows. As she moves to get off the table she sees the dry piece laid out there, still folded in the shape of her body from where he wrapped it around her.

Delicately, delicately, she withdraws herself from it. She rises from the table and starts walking towards the shape standing at the window, walking towards him, unbidden, uncalled, she is walking to where he stands, or sleeps.

But there is nothing there.

And it is so late that there's darkness in the room and the market outside is closed . . . In the restaurants and bars they have put the chairs up on the tables, the shops have the shutters pulled down, the street light on the corner flickers.

But still she goes closer, closer to the window, with pain still in her, fluid falling from her eye, from cuts, down her legs, and she half walks, as if to him, through him, through his shape that is a shadow, walking through dark air, and she stands against the glass, lets the glass hold her hot skin with its cool clean face, lets it hold her but the weight of her body . . . Her insides are coming down.

I remember, my mother lay upon the sofa in the dark.
Her long red hair hung down like a cloth.
As a child I watched over her, I waited . . .

And it seems as if she waits for the sirens now, coming for her like she waited the other time, and there is one open eye, one closed eye, the sirens coming for her and the mess of her death all over the hard floor . . .

But it's not the same, it's not the same.

She holds her stomach, she waits at the window with her insides coming down, she waits at the window like a little girl, like before, but not like before . . . Death already left the room, he has gone.

Third Part

The Opening Glass

ONE

My mother knew the night she met my father: *This is the man I will marry*. She recognised him by his cruelty, in his black eyes, she knew him, in his red shining lips, the fingers in a circlet of bone around her arm . . . She knew when she first saw him that she wouldn't be able to run from him, caught in a garden, behind high walls. She knew from the tone of his voice, even though she didn't understand most of the words, that it was a voice that would make the rules, that would be always close.

"Let me get you a drink . . ."

Like before.

I can see her, dressing in her room at home, preparing herself to see him again. Smoothing down her slip, drawing on her lipstick in the mirror . . . Thinking with each gesture about that first night. How he took her elbow and steered her towards the bar and how she expected it. How she always knew she would meet him, that there would be a man at the party who would become a lover for her, who would draw her in.

"Excuse me . . ." he said.

And she looked up.

"I feel I know you too . . ."

She remembers now, as she completes her lipstick mouth in the mirror, how his lips parted for her in a smile that night, because, she knew, it was the reply he wanted.

"I feel I know you too . . ."

And she feels so clever that she knew.

All the other times, in the summer, when she had left the cottage to dance with boys at the tennis club, in lit marquees that were like frail lanterns in the darkness, the silhouettes of boys showing through the thin cloth, fluttering shadows on the grass, and before, when she had visited cocktail parties with her father as his partner, with his arm around her . . . No time was like this evening when she is ready, in her girl's room for the last time, ready, all in a piece to be a bride.

When her father had driven her to parties in his long steel-grey car, when he had taken her, introduced her, then there had been that sense of a shameful thing, too intimate for a girl. Now at last, it will not be him with her powder showing on his dark jacket, not him getting her drinks from the bar . . . Though it feels like him, the hand at her back, it is not him. Her heart isn't full up in her like those other times. She does not have to feel the weight of her dress, the cut of it made to show the shape of her breasts, stitched closely to her waist so he can put his hand there, run his finger along the tiny raised silk seam.

She was always aware of people watching them together – that they could see the size of her waist by the way the father held her when they danced. When he put his large hand on the small of her back and pressed her to him, she was aware that they could see how small she was, how huge he . . . That they used to watch her with pity, not speaking, that they couldn't take their eyes off this awful thing . . .

But this evening it will change, she will make it different from before. They will not watch her . . . She will make it that way.

This night, when she leaves her father for the last time, she thinks they will never watch her again . . .

Gently she opens the long window in her bedroom.

The sash slides up with no sound, then a little wider, enough for her. With her satin shoes held in one hand, she uses the other to lever herself over the window-ledge out onto the branch of the pear-tree that grows outside her bedroom window. It is late summer and small fruits have started to grow amongst the thick fans of leaves, they brush against her arms. In her bare feet she steps along the first branch, clasps the rough bark overhead with her free hand, and, with the hand holding the shoes, she hitches up a filmy length of her skirt, high, lifting it clear up off her bare legs, to step up to a better branch where she's more secure.

No one can see her here in her lovely tree, amongst the leaves. She is safe. She tosses her shoes, like a little girl, down onto the smooth cropped lawn below. Then, with her expensive gown still gathered up in a pile around her she slides down the trunk of the beloved tree and jumps down into the cool evening grass where her white slippers lie tumbled. She puts them on at once so she can be ready to leave.

She dare not look back at the house, at the dark windows of her father's room, at all the dark windows . . .

She dare not look.

She will not let herself feel she is betraying.

Even fully dressed, in the beautiful long white dress of silk he gave her, in the dainty fitted shoes that have hundreds of tiny beads sewn onto them, in the strap of milky pearls she wears around her throat, in her ears, in all the pieces she wears, even the scented underwear lying close to her, though all these things are given by her father (*Take these, take these . . .*), still she will not let herself feel she is betraying. Even with the memory of him handing the heavy card boxes to her, the things inside filmed with tissue and with scent . . . Though this memory is in her, her father's dark searching eyes, poor hungry eyes as she unwraps the gifts (*Take these, please, take these . . .*), the dress, the tiny light shoes . . . Still, she on this night will not feel she is betraying; there will be no shame. She is leaving. It is the fact, the grain, like a stitch in the hem of her skirt. The only thing without which all the rest will become undone . . . It's in her heart. She can make herself believe her dress this evening is a final act of love for the father she is leaving, but already, standing here alone in the green, he feels far away.

The summer evening is clear and light, the last day's sun all around her, in the gold new-forming fruits in the tree, in the scent of newly mown grass at her feet . . . With all this beauty around her she is ready to leave the darkness of him.

Dressed in the clothes he has given her she turns, kisses the pear-tree at the trunk, then runs lightly from her father's garden without looking back . . .

I think of my mother often as that girl. I think of her breath, of her light footsteps across the lawn. I think of the way the last of the sun must have caught her that night, in the golden garden, then, later, standing with the other girls at the party, all their crystal glasses glittering but only one to catch brightness for my father, who saw her and decided then that tonight would be the last of the parties, that they would go away.

I think of those early meetings, how she turned to meet him, and she turned and she turned. There was the gleam of lights, like sugar. There was a shining interior with mirrors that reflected a hundred faces, the man's touch on the woman's arm.

And she smiles for him, the young woman smiles because she knows, the first night, the last night, all the nights: *This is the man I will marry.*

There is no one else.

Before, all those times in the summer, when a boy brought her back to the cottage, though she was alone then, her father was always there.

She could sense him, like breath on her neck, like the movement of his finger on the ridge of cloth. He laid claim from the outset, so the boys who brought her home afterwards would feel inexpert and shy to themselves when they tried to kiss. The sea edge was white at their backs in the moonlight but their hands were heavy in her hair and lap to spoil it . . . And all the time there was that other man, across the garden, waiting for her. Behind the dark window, inside the dark room, waiting, while the sigh of the sea was every-where, and the scent of the summer air and the garden . . .

As the boy tried to press nearer to her, tried to put his tongue whole into her mouth . . . All my mother could do, too shaped by a particular desire to let herself be free in the open air, was draw back her thoughts to that dark room in the house behind the hedge, it was her house, the place where she lived . . . And her father, standing inside the house where she lived, was waiting, thinking that she was out there on the lawn . . . Thinking her dress was coming off in the boy's hands, thinking she was letting herself be touched and smoothed, letting herself be looked at . . .

For so long she believed when her father said she was frail, like her mother had been frail, without him encircling her waist how lost she would be, and empty . . . She believed she could never go out without him. But when at last she did leave his house, when she let herself out through the open window into her tall tree, she didn't feel like a child, or a sick woman.

She opened her mouth wide when my father came down.

Of course, it is no surprise she was so quickly taken. When I think of her small excitements, with her first lover's kisses and no one to watch them do it . . . For my mother, this was real life.

She was with other people who smiled and talked, who were inquisitive about other things; they did not look at her. She could let

174

herself be held, taken around the room for dancing, she could be surrounded by the movement and soft colours of dresses, the folds of her own dress slipping against her legs, and the room whirling for her round and around like a beautiful carousel . . . Her father was not there and she was light without him, open to the world as a flower.

As the swirl of pastel dresses joined and parted and joined again in a dance behind her, she felt for the first time to be part of the dance, like everyone in the world was in it. She moved amongst the shifting pattern of pink and lemon and violet, she let the delicate edges of silk and tulle and lace touch, settle. Each moment was air that belonged to her.

It was inevitable she would be picked, fate.

Picked, to be arranged, to have her drink prepared for her . . . It was what she was used to. Though the man who chose her was not gentle with her, and though she couldn't understand him, his foreign tongue curling, and his lips at her ear forming words that made no sense, still, my mother responded to him as though she were a bloom and he had watered her.

She looked up into his dark face when he handed her the drink he had fetched, with gratitude, like open petals to his face, all her petals foolishly showing to him.

"I feel I have known you all my life . . ."

That is what I see now, looking back, that everything had to be familiar to her. She was a woman who knew nothing, who smiled open mouthed through a ball where everyone else wore painted lips, masks . . . Who didn't know better, who thought it all a costume, that the men outfitted in uniforms and paper medals really could protect her . . . She thought she was no different from the rest when I see how she behaved that night, like a child, like her father said, because she knew no other way . . . Her head turning, like a child, looking at everything, taken in by a man who was just like the one she already knew.

"I know you . . ."

"I know you . . ."

Who, like him, could snap her at the stem.

Poor mother, you never learned that you could never really escape, that the night you stepped out the window to your first party, into the branches of the pear-tree outside the window, you were not leaving. You could never be alone. Never could you have sat quietly, let people speak to you, learn who you were. Never could you be trusting enough in yourself to learn how to live.

I want to believe that it could have been different for you, for myself I want to believe it. That you could have let yourself grow up, away from your father, that you could have left him behind forever that night. I need to believe it was possible for you to begin again, find a life that was your own and you could keep it . . .

But instead you ran straight into the arms of another father. Like all the frightened women who run frantically towards the future and all they meet is memory . . . You knew nothing. With your dress damp in the starlight, and all undone.

T w o

When they came back to the city the husband kept his new wife inside, far away from her father, and his house with the high walls.

He kept her inside the rented room they shared, and she didn't need to think about her father ever again now there was this one man for her, only him.

It was winter then. When my father came home to her at night, he would turn the radio on for reports of the weather outside closing down the city. There were news stories about cars bound in the road by snow, the hard slick of water frozen to ice in the black gutters. My mother imagined the hush of white outside, with snow deep in every crevice, and she drew the sheet up around her throat. The sheet had to be enough, there was nothing else in the room for warmth, but it wasn't enough. My father had to bring vodka to her, tip it down her throat, to revive her.

Sometimes when he came home he was drunk and his voice was slurred and then he would open her mouth using the neck of the bottle for leverage. He tipped back her head with the bottle and poured the drink in. His eyes had become nearly closed with the alcohol, the lids as if they were scraped of skin. My mother was such a young bride. She had never seen him like this before, and she was trying to comfort him, but they were both ill with the cold and the weather.

He coughed and coughed all through the nights. He knew by then there was to be no more money from her.

"It was just that it was winter . . ." my mother tried to say to me. "That was all, it was winter. We were together, that's the important thing . . ." she tried to say, "the most important thing . . ."

But her husband coughed again. And sometimes there were specks of yellow left at the corner of his mouth and he didn't clean them away.

They had not been back in the country for more than a few weeks and he was no longer in love with her. All the talk he used to give her late at night, as they lay in a narrow bed together, all the pretty speeches for love, in languages she never understood . . . That had stopped. He just wanted her with vodka in her, he wanted her eyes rolling, to stop the hungry love eyes, he wanted to close them. No more love, only the radio on for words.

She was ridiculous to him she was so young.

"Darling . . ." She tried to speak but he forced the neck of the bottle inside her mouth, pushing it in, tipping her head right back.
"Drink . . ."
And my mother closed her eyes, she was so stupid for him in

love. She smiled her poor little crazy smile because she would never leave him.

"Darling . . ."

Her cheeks were flushed.

"Darling . . ." she said, and her voice was high, a foolish little voice.

"Darling . . ."

It was the only thing she could say.

"Darling . . ."

Like a doll.

For this reason of course she had no other thoughts left in her for a father. He could be wasting to bone behind his high walls, but he was a stranger to her by then. She never had to think about him, dream about him. Though, years later, lying on her sofa, she would feel regret for that first man, formed in tears, though she knew he died lonely, too full of his unspent heart . . . Still she never missed him. Sometimes she would feel a kind of sadness for his poor hands coming for her in her girl's bedroom, coming for her little girl's night-dress that he loved, the pretty trim, the lace, but in the end, the memory of his hands was always too big, his big head coming up close to her in the dark . . .

"Let's just see if this little lace piece will come undone . . ."

And then she forgot about him again.

Her father died knowing he had lost his daughter the night she ran out of the party into the moist air. He knew then. Not that he had lost her to a man, to a lover. He had taken all of her for himself so there could be nobody else . . . He was the only one. He had required of her too much, needed her too much, and in the end the weight of that knowledge had become a growth in him that was all he knew. He waited and waited for her that last night, before he went upstairs to unlock the drawer in his study. But he knew before dawn came, before his hands even touched the revolver, that he was the one, not his daughter's simple desire, to blame. He was the one who had made her go.

Isn't it the way all family stories turn, the same wheel bringing death to one another from love, brokenness from need? My mother, my father . . . They were not so different from the rest. Love is too close, in a family it is much too close, it presses in. There is the familiarity of goodnight kisses, sweet foods eaten off the same spoon, the insistence of old lips to young mouths. There are fresh looks in the morning, a glimpse of a child stepping from her bath, the parent's outstretched arms to hold the small wet body . . . Love is too much in a family, it is always too close. It makes, of a mistaken touch in the dark, fate, the thing intended.

For my mother, there was no way out: she was stifled in airless rooms, motionless in still gardens. Though she tried to leave, as her father believed she had left him, she came back to the same close rooms, the same people. Years later a new set of characters may fill up space in the room, may live in some city or other, over time, or leave, or arrive . . . But in the end it was all the same. There was the pressure of the dark sliding over against the light, the same close smell.

Yet when I see in my mind's eye the way my father took her

back to his dark house, and there, in the hallways, stripped her bare
of her clothes in the cold . . .

When I think how compliant she must have been with him, soft,
her hair down over her face, and not moving while all the time he
pushed his old body closer into hers, closer so she could feel his
dryness rasp and move, the lips, the smell . . .

"Darling . . ."

And when I see my father with my mother, with her pushed up
against the wall, and his breath coming ragged, when I think of the
way his hands expertly shift her against the wall . . .

"Upstairs . . ."

When I think of his muttering, because he wants her in the bed
now, and him on top of her . . .

"Upstairs . . ."

When I think about the foolish smile on her face when he gave
her attention, for the easy way she bent to him, let her arms and
legs be bound for him . . .

When I see how the table was brought out for me, and there was
something on the table, and it was dark, I couldn't see, but when he
laid me down on the skin my mother used to keep, and I felt it,
under me, touching me . . . When I think . . .

There, there . . .

The prickling hairs, the familiar thing . . .

There, there . . .

Then – "No!"

"No!"

"No!"
"No!"

Like I screamed that night, and the familiar thing fled.

Like waking up suddenly in the dark alone, and with the cry out of sleep, wakefulness comes, the dream gone.

THREE

See how dark the room has become, how the dusk has come in and brought night behind it like a shadow.

See how the black window shines.

He has left her alone to go out, to find men, or women, whatever he does when he leaves her . . . He won't be back tonight. Through the window she sees the street light come on, neon lights from the bar down the road, yellow from an Egyptian café on the corner.

She rolls over on the cheap and narrow bed, but now she won't sleep again. Her body is sticky with dirt. Yet she cannot get up to bathe, cannot get up to her bathroom, to see, in the mirror there, the horrible thing she has become.

The city is too full of memories for her now, the streets where he put his arm around her, the places where he fed her. There is nowhere else left.

The man is out.

Before, he used to bring the people home who he met at night, they were his friends. For a time, she used to know them. She used to prepare the tray like wives do prepare, with the glasses on it, a tray of crystal seedlings, and a bottle. She poured the drinks for the black-haired men who sat with her husband, late into the night. She went about the room with the tray, trembling, as she moved amongst her husband's friends. The tray with the crystal shimmered. As she took each drink, not speaking because no one in the room spoke English for her, the only sound she made was the trembling shimmer of the glass. She was a maid, her head was down. When she served her husband vodka and caviare from a dish with a tiny spoon, when he was in the company of his friends, he didn't look at her then.

Now he rarely looks at her.

Only later, when they had all gone home, did my father reach for my mother with her tray, and by then it was dirtied with ash, left bits of food. There were soiled cigarette ends on it, used glasses . . . And he reached for her when she was exhausted, but still she had been waiting for him to do it, all the time she was his little waitress. Waiting while men sang for him, drank. Waiting while small women sat on her husband's knee, whispered in his ear and he laughed, pinched them.

My mother was exhausted by the noise, the movement, the large bodies of the men, the sweet heavy fragrance of the women in her room . . . So when he came to her it was too late, her hands raw from the soapy dishwater, cut from the glasses they had broken which she, on her hands and knees, had cleared from the floor.

Her pretty hands were spoiled, and her body, from the way he had used her . . . But still he reached for her and though it was too late for her she let him; she was grateful. Glad as he reached behind her and drunkenly undid the ties from her apron, as he reached for his maid who stood quietly as her husband, excited more and more by how he has ruined her beauty, undressed her, clumsily pulling away her clothes. After he had her, quickly and with violence while she stood upright, not moving, while she stood in the centre of the room after he'd pulled up his pants, the party mess all at her back, at her feet, then he went to sleep. His body filled up the bed.

By now, this is how her addiction is fixed in her: humiliation and desire the line she will continue. Soon he will leave her. It will be the night he goes out for cigarettes, he won't come back but even then she will continue.

And, like her, it seemed I would continue, lying quietly in hospitals, like she lay, in rooms, waiting for the moment when her life would become my life, each part so fitted a stranger could not see where one edge merged with the other. For so many years my mother's stories were me, they were the only thing I knew, to continue her line, to continue . . . Like she was born, so was I, to recognise looks, touches. To know exactly the way a man would make her feel when he took her out to bars late at night, when he pretended to the other men there that she was his daughter and he would sell her – let them put their hands up her skirt to try.

The men smiled sly smiles at him, narrowed their eyes, not quite believing him, but still came near, their fingers twitching, their eyes filmy and their breath of onions, rusty water, on her face.

My mother closes her eyes. The pear-tree is gone. Her white dress is gone.

A Story Known by Heart

After the dark night I stayed in the room at the top of the house but it was not the same as before.

The man slept, drank, slept again. Sometimes I heard him moving in the house, looking for fresh bottles. Then it was quiet. He came back into the room but did nothing. He simply pulled back the sheet and came in beside me, as if I could give him some warmth.

More and more he was tired, too overwrought to keep on like before. Days passed and he slept with an exhaustion that came from deep within him, his breath coursing through his body and his dark mouth wide open for air.

I should not be surprised. He had always been such an old man.

I remember when he kissed me the first time, how even then his lips felt like they had no moisture in them, no flesh. He leaned across the marble table, across the plate of iced cakes. He touched my cheek and his old finger was shy as a moth on my skin. And after all the months that passed, still, whenever he began, I could always feel that little kind of fear in him, that tremble in his hands, because he thought that this may be the last time for him, with his poisoned breath. The last time, with the pains that pulled on him, drew like acid, the minute his desire took hold.

At first I wanted to go to him, stroke his hard face, to comfort him. I wanted to put my fingers in his dry hair, use my fingers to part the dryness to his scalp, run my fingertip down the line. The dye had stained the line black but as I would touch him in the darkness I would see that the soft old piece at the nape of his neck was still white like a baby. But as time passed not even his vanity kept me. I didn't want even that most tender thing.

Winter had passed by now, yet every day it became colder. In the streets, in my white sheets there was cold. The old man slept beside me, and still I lay beside him, quietly, listening.

Outside the window, down below on the street there was the movement of shapes in the dark, warm breath. Nothing else sounded in the room. The air from the man's breath grew lighter, with no shift or sigh. There was no love or seed left in him, only this sound, soft clap of hoofs in the snow, shapes gathering in the dark.

Another morning passed, and another, morning into morning, white with dawn and cold, and every morning I heard the horses come, I could hear them outside the window, and later, as I lay awake and listened, I could hear the men who kept the horses. I could hear their boots.

They came with carts and metal bars to erect their market stalls, with wrenches, with bolts. Through the thick glass of the high bedroom I could hear them in the street below, the low tones of their talk early in the morning, the way they were so urgent with each other, their harsh voices and the sound of their boots scraping the pavement, the screw of iron, hammer's bang.

They talked together as I lay in bed. In an empty street, they were each deciding where to put his cart, his stand. Here vegetables, and here for meat, the barrel of bones. Here the place for the bleach cart, with mops and dusters, for flowers. For fruit, paper sacks of sugar candies. I heard them swear as they set up their stalls, and I heard them fight, I heard their scurfing boots.

I started getting out of bed when I heard them come. The sick man never wakened. It was so early my breath puffed white at the window glass. It was cold and the window was like a piece of ice, but still I stayed there, looking down into the unlit street, past the big bodies of men, to where I saw the horses, moving, shifting, their soft shapes humped together in the morning darkness.

They were not young; though they were colours – white and brown, black – in the early light they had no colour. They were market horses, geldings and deformed from work. Their backs were buckled, the spine bent from pulling market wagons of bars and high wooden crates, from dragging the carts filled with root vegetables packed with clods of dirt. The bits had been left in their mouths for so long, and the harnesses on their backs, that they did not remind them of labour. There was never anything other than this.

Every morning after I heard the men come, I went to the window to look for the horses. There was the slow switch of the tail, slow rhythmic chewing. I saw one horse apart from the rest, his head down in a sack, eating the dry stuff that was put there. He made no sound. Tinder bits fell on the ground around him as he chewed, the metal shifting in his mouth, wooden shafts low across his back. He swung his head and the tail of another horse touched him.

Another touched, and another.

All the way up and down the road, where the men left them to unload their carts, I saw the worn brown and grey and dirty white heads of horses. No matter how old, or tired, the curve of their bowed necks made them seem contented to me, as if they had chosen to be there.

At my back, the man rasped, he gagged in his sleep. Then he was silent again. More and more he was sleeping.

I could stand at the window for hours, if I wanted, I could do anything at all. Eat food he had brought for himself but now it was mine. Replace under the covers the hand that was so light it was like a paper hand hanging from the bed.

Or I could leave him, I could go downstairs and dress myself in clothes I found in boxes in the hall, and walk out the front door.

There, there . . .

I would whisper to him, so he would not know that I was leaving.

There, there . . .

I imagined that I would quietly open the front door so no one would hear, push it softly behind me.

And I would be outside, stepped out into the cold air, out into the road. It would be so cold I wouldn't even feel my body, but the breath of horses would be warm.

I would walk over to where the brown horse was eating and reach out, put my hand on his neck. He wouldn't even feel me. He wouldn't look up, or shake his head. I would be so gentle with him in the cold it would be as if I was invisible. Voices wouldn't come near, or the sound of boots. There would be the lovely calm of a horse eating, that would be all, steam coming from his breath, his nostrils, warm air rising from his flank. I would pass my hand over the rough surface of his skin and smooth it, imagine my hand making him lovely again.

There, there . . .

I would run my hand along his side. And I would feel myself, in the lovely, smoothing, burnishing gesture, to be a child again, my palms pressed down upon the skin my mother kept, and the dense brown hairs flattened out between my fingers as I stroked over and over, making the skin warm and the surface soft like oil.

Easy, now . . .
Gentle . . .

Like it could be alive again.

The hairs were brown and dry, and from the yellowed bits that still clung onto it like meat I knew that it had been taken straight from the animal after killing.

There, there . . .

I used to stroke it, care for it.
Easy, now . . .

But that was a long time ago, and here would be a real horse to touch, not a flat shape laid out on a sofa or bed for a young woman to lie upon. I would be able to feel the lovely shivering map of muscles and veins beneath the skin, the ridges of bone and cartilage and sinew.
There, there . . .

I could stand with my hands upon the horse and he would let me. There would be the calm rhythm of his eating, and his warm, sweet-smelling breath. Loosely I would put my arms around his neck, let my face rest against him there, against that calm side.

I could let my cheek rest against the warmth of his worn tobacco neck, his dark wet eye near my own.

The light in the room was changing.

I stayed in the room, with the dry, papery face of the old man laid out on my pillow, but the sun coloured the walls earlier than before. Time was shifting, moving on.

"There, there . . ." sometimes I whispered to him.

"Easy . . ."

He would be dead soon.

He no longer left the bed for food or drink, he lay quietly. His breath came slowly in shallow rafts from deep within his hollow body. He didn't move.

As the weeks went on more and more I left him on his own. I was going through the house for food and clothes, I stopped sleeping beside him in the bed.

"Darling . . ."

Sometimes he tried to speak, but I stayed at the window.

"*Meu doce* . . ."

I saw myself instead outside with the horses, with people in the street around me.

"Darling . . ."

More and more I knew, through the glass: *This is how the story ends . . .*

There was the knife in at the base of the backbone, pushed under and spread like a knife spreading paint across a plate, spreading wide the flank, spread enough to give an edge to catch between thumb and fingers . . .

There the whole dark glossy pelt ripped away from the wet flesh with one great red sucking sound, moist flesh separated from moist flesh, the whole piece lifted in a great flap from the body, a glossy, bleeding cape, dark and black and still warm, lined in a silk of blood . . .

I touched it.

The dry hairs, the worn yellow underside.

Downstairs, in the boxes in the hall, were all my mother's things. Her pretty rugs, in boxes the plates and silver she'd eaten from once, the pearls she'd worn around her throat. In chests and crates had been collected all the possessions that had been hers. Everything she had was stored in that dark hall except the one thing which was the gift that had been made to her, the last part of the story left to tell.

That part was here with me.

———————

I see my mother now, lying back on her sofa, and the animal skin is upon it.

That's better, now . . . Darling, don't look at me.
Run away and play and let mummy dream . . .

I see her for the last time, in the small room we shared when I was a child. She lies back on the sofa with her long red hair, asleep on the animal skin, but she's not sleeping.

There, there . . .

Her hair falls down upon the skin.

She lies on the sofa and dreams.

In the first dream she stands on the blue lawn in early evening. In one hand she holds the frail glass, in the other, petals, a rose already blown her father has given her as a gift. She feels the confusion of him, his moving eyes, the way his hand trembles when he pours the drinks, in his fragrant rose-head pressed into her palm. He claims her with such grace and manner, he is cunning with her, but his poor eyes . . . He is frightened of her too. Though he has been using her since she was a little girl, for years using his daughter's body, whispering his sorry words into the tiny opening of her ear, though he has woken her in the middle of the night, when she feels his hands suddenly on the bedcovers, passing over her . . .

"It's Daddy, darling. It's our game."

She opens her eyes, sees his face up close to hers.

"Darling, I love you very much."

. . . There were always his frightened eyes, the starving eyes.

Now she is a young woman and so much time has passed but nothing has changed. In the dream she stands on the lawn thinking about him, she still lives here with him, the same high garden walls surround them on a summer evening. Pressed petals line her closed fist. The scent of them comes up. In her throat the thick sweet of the drink he has made her swallow.

"This now, this . . ."

He holds the crystal rim to her lips, tips back her head, pours the sweet liquid in.

"Good girl . . ."

She dreams, and now another evening shows itself to her in pictures behind her closed eyes. There's a mirror, a man's dark arm, a white dress printed against the dusk . . . A man holds her close.

"Look at yourself . . ."

He holds her at the mirror, holds her there. She sees her own red lips reflected in the glass, not a man, only the red of her lips, parted, then her mouth opening wider, wider.

These are her real dreams and she wants sleep to come to take the dreams away. She is losing weight quickly now. When she looks down the length of her body the bones of her pelvis are like part of the boat she lies in, her arms the oars, her ribs are the curved side of her small boat, the part that will feel water.

She lies, in a flat calm on her sofa in the darkened room. The dreams are real. There's nothing in her but two men have allowed them: pieces of soft food, his thin acid semen, her own blood that he has wiped back in. Nothing else, the white bones of the boat is all. She dreams she could not keep a baby hooked inside her if she wanted it for the journey, she has no flesh for it to hold, no muscle in her vessel to tie it. She is light. I know, the breasts are gone, they could not give milk. The lover has taken them, I know, the puppet, burnt them, like her womb, only black stuff is there, no bloody rag to give birth to. No thing to come out now that the puppet has been in.

My mother shifts in sleep, then settles. She sees the axe, the look in her husband's eye. She thought he was riding, she thought, for seconds, the horse was rearing . . .

There, there . . .

She thought the red was streamers, something her husband carried.

There, there . . .

*

198

She thought the creature's screams were pleasure.

No!

It took her seconds, minutes, to understand. And then, running across the green field, the blades of grass jewelled with blood, the creature's rolling eye . . . And then the thing was already done.

No!

She wakes, there's a child at the window, it's her child.

Outside in the market, the men and women who kept the stalls brought out all their horses. I watched them lead them out from the stables in the old mews, lead them down the street, quietly in the early morning light.

None one of these sad horses had glossy skin lain upon their backs, they had no skin worthy of raiment, for a new bride. These horses had tired hoofs, they would always submit to the harness, the bit. Their worn shoulders were blistered in parts from the wooden shaft of the cart.

None of them were near in beauty and in size and power to the huge black creature my father slaughtered for my mother that day. None of these poor animals, huddled together in the market street, their carts loaded with unsold vegetables, would bring to mind the bright afternoon my father drew my mother into a field.

"A picnic," he had told her, as they drove out of town on a day in early spring. The sky was high and proud and pale blue, with no clouds. The blue shone like polished china, green checkered hills rising up on either side of the road, all the fields bright tablecloths for picnics spread out wide under the clean sky.

"A picnic," he had told her, but in the car there was an axe lying across the back seat.

"I want to make a surprise for you. Something that will make you keep me forever . . ."

Nothing I saw through the glass in my high room resembled the black animal chasing a light scent in the spring air, flicking back and forth along the fenceline that came up close beside the part of the road where my father stopped the car.

That black horse was a whip, back and forth, back and forth. The muscles and hair and black skin of that animal flicked and turned and switched in the bright light. None of the grey market horses resembled the violent motion of that black animal, screeching into the hot blue sky that it had been penned in, that it had been kept, when it was unbroken, ungelded, the energy of blood and sex running down the length of the black body.

No!

It screamed into the blue air.

No!

*

200

I see it screeching along the fenceline once more, then it stops its course, stands still.

In the quiet centre of the blue, my father's hand closes around the wooden handle of his axe. In dead quiet he softly opens the car door, his thumb stroking the smooth wood.

My mother's breath is like gauze.

She sits in the car, she doesn't know what he is doing. She watches as he creeps up to the horse where it stands, to steady it, the weapon at his side like it's a gentle thing, like something so gentle that he would use it to slice grass for the animal, or clumps of clover, so gentle that my mother would never guess, once my father has mounted the dark horse how he would use the bone handle, the thick blade.

"There, there . . ."

Everything I need for the end of my story is here.

If I stood at the window for hours to see my rows of pale horses being led down the street, if I looked through glass into the crowded neighbourhood where I grew up, there would be nothing to compare with the strength and light of that day, the empty forgotten fields. With the tiredness, the worn skin of a workhorse and the shining pass of that untempered unbroken blackness, nothing. Nothing in a city like the still blue air that contained only an animal's sound.

All my mother's life was in that day, the pattern in her fixed. There were the ties of blood and family turning neatly into desire, that twist, that intricate binding that goes for generations set up in that day to pattern in her, to repeat in me. There was the press of an old body to form the next generation, the design laid out like fingers of lovers interlacing, mother, father, daughter, and my fingers there amongst them, gathered up into the knot, the hand that is held.

Yet all the time it was happening, my poor mother didn't know a thing. She couldn't believe it wasn't a crop that my father was bringing down upon the animal's haunches, over and over, once he was mounted and running, not a switch he was bringing down at the horse's neck there, in the far corner of the field. Until she saw the horse fall she didn't know, thought the strange motion coming from the animal was from the passion of being mounted, didn't know that the red streaming down over the black skin, my father's hand on the axe shiny with red, the blade caught with banners of blood, that the gape at the animal's throat, was meat, sacrifice.

As she ran over the field towards my father she could smell the blood. In the air she could smell it, and could see it, too, in the look in his eye as he stood over the killed animal in the empty field.

In the still air she heard flies buzzing. Already flies were collecting around this huge thing he had done.

"For you . . . This is something for you . . ."

And from his pocket he took the skinning knife. In the bright light its shining blade reflected in her eyes and she couldn't see.

"Zhertva . . ." my father said.

"It is . . ." He didn't know the word.

202

"You must keep this . . ."

The words came out of him like knives, zhertva, seikrid, like cuts in the throat, the same words over and over.

"For you . . . For you . . ."

And he took up the blade and skinned the horse, and my mother had to watch, she had to stand there in the black wet grass, as he started at the base of the long backbone and slid the knife wide like he knew how, taking clean slides of the blade between the skin and flesh, and when he was done he lifted the light cotton dress my mother was wearing up over her shoulders, up over her golden body and he replaced upon her for clothing the heavy skin.

No!

Blood smeared my mother's bright golden skin, drops of red and long silks of red across her golden skin like sequins and beads, like embroidery.

No!

But my father smoothed all the blood down her, he wet her, under the heavy shining skin. He lay her down, together they lay down on the grass, they both of them smelled like death, and around them the flies buzzed and gathered as my father slit open his trousers and forced himself inside her, pushing himself in, deeper in, cramming himself in until in the wet bleeding grass she conceived and she pleased him then, when he did it, but it was the ending for him. He smiled at her, like, later all the old men would smile with dirty eyes. He was finished. He traced her lips with his thick blooded finger, smiling, the skin wet and hot on her while he began to touch her, pushing his thick blooded fingers between her lips, pushing deeper and deeper into her mouth, down into the back of her throat until she was sick.

"Querido . . ."

Flies buzzed around my mother's mouth.

"Darling . . ."

She had been so fragrant, and look at her now.

This is the ending of my mother's story for me, the sacrifice. When he said "Look at you . . ." that day.

"Look at you . . ."

And she looked back at him with eyes that were still believing.

Even after this monstrous thing, still believing, still believing it was a gift, the bleeding cape on her shoulders a gift, like a white dress had been a gift, like all sacrifices are given as gifts that will start turning into death the moment they are accepted. Always she was still believing . . .

She was a little girl, she was always such a little girl.

She let herself be wrapped in the freshly killed skin as if it was a lovely thing, a gift, the keepsake she always said it was, because she could only believe in gifts, only lovely stories . . . And this is why, I know now, for so long I had no story of my own. Because I thought my mother's life was my life, something to be told over and over until the words became my own, when all the time she did not really know her own story, she was too afraid to tell it. And I am here, years later, and I have let myself live out her life, told her story entire so even the ending is in me, and it is why for so long I had no story of my own. Because the ending of my mother's story is the beginning of my own.

Every morning the men came, and I continued to wait for them, every day the same.

They were unloading their carts, and their horses stood by while the men unlatched the carts and lifted the boxes and crates from them, the vegetables, the carrots and the onions and the cartons of fruit. I saw the rafts of oranges come out, I saw a box of apples tumble from a man's arms. They fell from him in slow motion, tumbling softly around the bumpy surface of the road. Apples into gutters, apples down the street, under cars, into the drains, green apples, their colour reminded me of spring leaves. So many apples they fell and rolled and scattered like green buttons from a tin, like round green seeds sprinkled on the cold ground for a new season.

The mornings came very early now, wisps of cloud showed in a blue sky. The dying man was getting colder but the room warmed for me. Sun came through the window where I stood and my blood became thicker, stronger, in the heat.

For weeks I had not slept with the cold body, I found blankets downstairs and made up a bed for myself apart from him, where I could close my eyes. I had found food, that was delicious to eat, chocolate, and cans of sticky drink, and sometimes I tried to feed the old man, pushing soft pieces I had chewed for him into his mouth, closing his lips together with my fingers so he would have to swallow. Mostly though, I kept the food for myself. I needed it more than him.

Outside, as the mornings deepened into days, the scraping, turning sound of iron bars stopped, the metal joints smoothed over with grease and the fabric coverings of the market stands were neatly fitted. It was the time when the men finished their work and the morning bars along the road were open, and there would be women inside for them, waiting. Loose eggs would slide into a pan for them, sugar would be mixed with milk at the bottom of a cup. The hot women at the cooker would cut sausages clean into white plates, would strip ham rind and gristle with their slick pink fingers.

As I thought about these things it became as if I was there with them. As if I could smell the fug of their cigarettes rising with the smoke of bacon fat and tea steam, as if I could taste, with the men's mouths, like I was sitting there with them at formica tables mopping up yellow yolks and red sauce with bread, standing outside with tea in a paper cup.

Through the window I saw men huddled by their stands, in shop windows, along the road. By now, the market had formed shape around them. The stalls were in place, and most of them were covered with plastic roofing, half-unpacked boxes beside. Some had red striped tarpaulins draped across their tops like so many little circus roofs, or there was green canvas, or blue plastic to protect against the rain.

More and more I was remembering, these things I knew, remembered.

There was the stand for exotic vegetables and the dark man who tended it, next to him the old lady who was freed from an asylum so she could come back to the market and sell. She was always the proud one that owned the prettiest apples, who would bring out a shy hand of bananas from behind her back. I remembered she used to sing a little song to herself as her hands fluttered over the apples, touching them quickly every so often, just to be sure they were still there.

"It's all I sell, and it's all I want to sell.

It's my own place and I'll do as I please.

Do you have a nice face? Are your feet clean?

Then I may say hello . . ."

Though I couldn't see her from my high window it was as if she was close. Like all the people were close. I knew these streets, this was where I used to live. When I was a child people in the market used to fill paper bags for me with sandwiches and fruit that I could take to school. They gave me vegetables and tins of cooked food. They wrapped sweets in twists of paper and slipped them in my pocket.

I remembered going to visit the potato man with his giant drum full of earth. He delved into it and brought out purple potatoes and huge knotted white potatoes stuck with eyes. Some had thin grey skins you could see the flesh through, and others were so thickly crusted with dirt they looked like clods of dried mud. There were potatoes heavy as men's fists that I could not have managed to take into my small basket. I used to count out the change and the man took it from me with his big forefinger and thumb.

"Thank you, miss. And I hope I'll be seeing you again . . ."

One by one all these details were coming back, forming fully in my mind. The places where I used to stand and walk and run. I heard a man roller-blade over a bump on the pavement, a child shriek when a dog sniffed the hem of her coat. I heard the slow movement of the Moroccan women passing in the street, the exchange of their long garments, one against the other, the rustle of a newspaper package that contained green mangoes.

More and more, these were the things that possessed me, these memories.

"Come to mummy, darling. There's a chocolate stain all down your new dress . . ."

More and more, these were the things that belonged to me.

"Fernand, can I ask you for a glass of water, the sugar in my coffee is very sweet."

"I see a lady, and I see a little girl."

"Yes, thank you, we are both very well. And what is best to have today? The sweet rolls? A cake? Please, choose for me. The cakes you pick from your shelf are always best."

For the first time in my own life I felt the weight, the shape and colour and texture of my own memories, details of things I alone knew, the bright pieces to take with me into age. I remembered, as something that belonged to me, the room my mother and I shared, and the smell of the room – a sweet mixture of the incense she sometimes burned, the sticks stuck in oranges for extra fragrance, and the blue smoke of cigarettes, the unstoppered bottles of expensive scent that lined the mantelpiece. For the first time the room was mine, like the memory of the clothes I wore then, the trims and buttons.

There was this place I used to visit, years ago, when I was a child, and later, when I was a young woman I loved it, a café where I could drink coffee and eat cakes. The owner was called Fernand and he looked after my mother in that café, later he looked after me.

I remembered the day I left the café for the last time, to go with an old man, to be led by him into his dark house. We walked by the coloured glass window for the last time, past the pretty colours created by light. For the last time I saw the wooden trays laid out with a thousand tiny sugar biscuits, cut in circles and stars and fingers, some broken, some crushed to crumbs. For the last time I smelled the sugar and egg from the pastry kitchen, for the last time was warmed by the heat of rising dough, freshly baked plait loaves.

Yet what happened to me then, many years ago now that I am like an old woman with these pages laid out smooth on my desk . . . It occurred because I had no other will. He was not forcing me indoors that day, he did not frighten me when he turned the key in the lock. When he asked for me in Fernand's café, when I went towards his table, when I looked into his black eyes, I knew. All my life was there, all my memory in his black eyes . . .

For a while, everything I needed was with him and his house was like a body for me, and I didn't move within it. I waited, with my hair down around my face, for days, for weeks I waited like my mother waited, for years, long ago, like so many people in locked rooms wait, their plates empty, waiting for someone who can come and make the story end.

And now, as I write, he is dying, a man in a high room above a market street, and every day as I tell his story there are less and less words.

There, there . . .

I stroke his paper skin.

The words left for him are getting thinner, lighter on the page, like his body, the bones showing through the white skin, torn in parts beneath his wrappings like soaked paper.

There, there . . .

By the end, I think, my mother must have known nothing she could do would make her husband stay.

Even that day when they made love in blood, when he laid the horse's hot stripped skin around her . . . By then he was so bored of her. So bored it took all his strength to ride the animal he wanted to kill. When he presented her with the thick hot skin, even while he was touching her, she was no longer alive to him.

In careful English he told her that he did love her, but I think her exhaustion began that day. The day was too bright, the sun too clear in the hard blue sky. She was exhausted by the thick air, the man's weight on top of her, exhausted by her conception, by the weight of slaughter . . . The smell of blood was in her hair and in her nostrils, caked blood on the backs of her thighs from where he had made her lie in the blood-soaked earth, blood on her shoulders from the garment of skin. They were all weights on her, she wanted to sleep. For a small minute she didn't care for him, only to sleep, and have the weight of him far away. If only she could hold onto her little handkerchief of sleep . . .

Instead, she opened her eyes.

Days later, with opened eyes she saw her husband pick up his jacket, walk out the door.

She rushed to him, she knew, she threw her arms around him, screaming, she stank of blood and flesh, the smell opened up with her tears. She screamed and pleaded to him not to go, but he simply unwound her arms from around his neck, used soothing noises with her like she was an animal, and when he had her calm on the sofa, when he had drawn up the skin around her for comfort, he left. He said he was going out for cigarettes.

Now, I take up that same skin. It cracks when I unfold it, but remains in one piece.

Over the frail person lying, sleeping, I place the skin, I draw it

211

up around his thin neck for comfort, smooth it down along his tiny body.

He will be dead soon.

Gone like my mother is gone, my father is gone. They won't come back again. The room where I stayed for a time, the dark house . . . Already it belongs to some other generation. The skin on my mother's sofa will be gone, and all the keepsakes, the little gloves and handkerchiefs and scraps of paper, all of these things have gone already, into dust, settling in patterns somewhere, in empty rooms, on suitcases and boxes in empty halls, dust instead of the things that once really did exist.

Dressed in my borrowed clothes I leave the room, go down the stairs, one flight then another. I pass all the long halls, past the locked doors and all the foolish things he keeps, packed in their piles along the walls, in crates and boxes like his life is here, but there is no life in this dark body.

Dust falls as I walk down, it settles, fills. It covers everything in a pale sheet, dust as dry and grey and ashy, dust as a person, dust everywhere, in my hair, under my nails. It's the dry taste in my mouth, dust falling out of me. All dust, my body, this empty room. Dust comes, covers. I am dust. I breathe dust. Let me be dust forever.

As I reach the front door, turn the key that is left in the lock, dust still falls behind me. In veils it falls and falls. As I step outside and turn to push the door I can't see the interior, only a grey square where once there was a hall, a house . . . Then nothing.

*

I walk along the road in sunshine so clear it hurts my eyes, but I know this warmth, this spring, I recognise the scent in the air, the streets, the thick wads of cherry blossom on the tree at the corner, the market gutters running with bright fragments of rubbish and spring melt.

I turn the corner and pass the house where I lived with my mother, years ago when I was a child. It is derelict now, and it seems strange I used to think it was beautiful. I walk further up the road and turn into the Portuguese café and the smell of sugar is warm in the warm air. I go inside and take a table by the window and Fernand comes to my table and he calls me by my name, no one else's name, not a father's name or a mother's name.

"It is good to see you" he says.

"We have missed you."

"But now you are here again, what can I get for you? What would you like?"

I sit by the glass window while he goes to bring me coffee and cake and I can't believe how clean the glass is, and shining in the spring light. I put my hand out to touch the glass and realise there is no window there, Fernand has opened wide the windows in the street to let in all the spring air. I put my arms out into the light, through where the glass was once, the sun is warm on my bare arms and I open my hands like I am receiving something from the air, fruit, piles of grain, opening my hands into the light and they are my own hands.

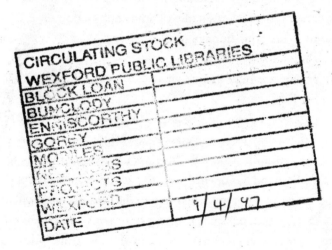